NANCY DREW

girl detective ™

#21

Close Encounters

CAROLYN KEENE

Aladdin Paperbacks
New York London Toronto Sydney

This book is a work of fiction. Any references to historical events, real people, or real locales are used fictitiously. Other names, characters, places, and incidents are the product of the author's imagination, and any resemblance to actual events or locales or persons, living or dead, is entirely coincidental.

❦ALADDIN PAPERBACKS
An imprint of Simon & Schuster Children's Publishing Division
1230 Avenue of the Americas, New York, NY 10020
Copyright © 2006 by Simon & Schuster, Inc.
All rights reserved, including the right of
reproduction in whole or in part in any form.
NANCY DREW is a registered trademark of Simon & Schuster, Inc.
ALADDIN PAPERBACKS, NANCY DREW: GIRL DETECTIVE, and
colophon are trademarks of Simon & Schuster, Inc.
Manufactured in the United States of America
First Aladdin Paperbacks edition December 2006
10 9 8
Library of Congress Control Number 2006922949
ISBN-13: 978-1-4169-1245-3
ISBN-10: 1-4169-1245-2

Winnie shrugged. "I ca~ ~ ~~~ up with the business. But it's too mu~ ~ ~ ~~ TV crew, the
media, and the in~ ~ ~ ~ ~ ~ ~ ~ ~
tion feels mo~ ~ ~ ~ ~ ~

"TV crew~ Bess repeated, and moved closer to the
window. "Is some new show set here?"

Mary Beth looked up from setting a table and
giggled. "You're kidding, right? Like, you haven't a
clue?"

For a moment Winnie looked at George, then threw
her hands up. "Of course. Why should you girls know
what's going on here? I guess the news hadn't hit River
Heights before you left town."

"What news?" George asked, sounding as impatient
as I felt.

Joel made a spooky theatrical sound, then grinned
sheepishly as Winnie warned him off with a hard look.
"They aren't from around here, Joel." She turned back
toward us. "It seems we've been invaded not just by
tourists—but by aliens."

NANCY DREW
girl detective™

Available from Aladdin Paperbacks

Contents

Out of This World

"**I love the smell** of Vermont in November!" my best friend Bess Marvin declared as I drove down the twisty mountain road. In spite of the chilly air, Bess had the window down and her long blond hair glinted in the afternoon sun.

"Personally I think it all looks a bit bleak," George Fayne remarked. George, Bess's cousin and my other best friend, was sitting behind us. Too leggy for the backseat, George shifted restlessly as she added, "This is primo downhill skiing country—and we're here too early to enjoy it."

I grinned to myself. Dark-haired George was definitely from the glass-half-empty side of the Fayne-Marvin family. "If it was ski season, your mom's friend Winnie couldn't have spared the time to visit with us," I told her. "My dad always says this is the time of year when all of Vermont looks like pumpkin pie. We should enjoy it."

"Pumpkin pie—now that's a thought," George said, immediately heartened by the prospect. "Winnie bakes a mean one. Hope she has it on the menu tonight." After cooking school Winnie Armond had opened a gourmet café in a small town in Vermont; Mrs. Fayne had become a caterer.

We were now on our way to visit Winnie, but I was beginning to wonder if we'd ever get there.

Scenic as the mountain road was, I was getting impatient. Had I taken a wrong turn back at the Burlington airport? And why was the traffic so heavy? I couldn't do much about the traffic, but I could check our directions.

Just when I was about to pull over and look at the map, Bess spotted a sign.

"You are now entering Brody's Junction, Vermont," she read aloud.

George cheered.

"All right!" I said. I hate being lost for long.

Bess took in the view. "Brody's Junction sure is worth the long drive. It's exactly like a Hollywood set for a New England country town!"

"If you edited out the traffic," George remarked.

"A real-time special effect—too bad you can't work

that kind of movie magic on your laptop!" I said. She took up the challenge good-naturedly. "When we get to Brody's Junction, I'll give it a try—or at least attempt to program a kill-the-traffic computer game."

After passing through a small covered bridge, we emerged in the heart of the town. Made up of mainly wooden two- and three-story buildings, Brody's Junction's main drag looked like tourist heaven.

Past the line of cars and SUVs, I spied the steeple of a white clapboard church rising above the tree-lined town square. Beyond the town lay steep-sided hills dotted with barns, silos, and cows. Looming over everything was a tall rugged mountain, its sides scarred with ski runs. Towers for the idle lifts glinted like gold in the afternoon light.

A state trooper directing traffic stopped us at a congested intersection.

"Here's a traffic mystery for you, Nancy," George teased. "Winnie said this was off-season. Why, then, all the cars?"

The suggestion made me laugh. "I hate to admit it, George, but when it comes to unraveling the riddle of traffic jams, even *I'm* clueless."

Maybe I should explain the mystery bit. My name is Nancy Drew, and back home in River Heights I have a rep as a pretty good amateur detective—solving real crimes and helping cops capture bad guys. My friends sometimes rib me about my tendency to land smack in the middle of a whodunit even when I'm on a shopping spree or just hanging with them and having fun.

Frankly, at the moment nothing about this quaint town seemed at all mysterious—except the traffic. I had to agree with Bess, the place did look like a movie-location scout's dream: Craft shops, art galleries, an ice cream parlor, bakeries, and upscale clothing boutiques lined each side of the street.

At the end of the next block I spotted a green and white awning. "George, that's the place—Winifred's Café—right?"

"Right," George answered. "She said there's extra parking behind the restaurant."

I flicked on my right-turn blinker and pulled into one of the few empty spots in the lot.

Like many of the other storefronts Winifred's Café was housed in a gleaming white clapboard building. Bay windows framed the entrance. The luscious aromas of something baking wafted out onto the street through the screen door.

"This place smells like heaven!" Bess remarked as she tried the handle on the door. In spite of a CLOSED sign the door opened to the jingle of little bells. A woman looked up from behind the counter. "We're closed . . . ," she started to say, then spotted George.

"George Fayne, I can't believe you're finally here! I had almost given up on you guys," she said. She hurried over, hugged George, and grinned warmly at Bess and me. She introduced herself as Winnie.

She was in her early forties, with the figure of a twenty-year-old, seriously curly dark hair, and a fresh, rosy complexion. Her brown eyes sparkled as she ushered us farther into the restaurant. A waiter was setting up the tables for dinner, and a young man in an apron was writing that night's specials on a chalkboard. He looked about the same age as Ned, my boyfriend back home. He was lanky with dark blond hair, and when he turned to greet us, I noticed his unusually large green eyes, framed with dark lashes.

Winnie introduced the man as Joel, her apprentice, and the waiter as Mary Beth. "I'm so glad you finally got here," Winnie said. "Better call your mom. I just got off the phone with her, and she's worried."

While George took her cell and phoned home, I decided it might be good to call my dad. He was glad to hear from me, but he hadn't expected me to phone home so soon. When my friends and I are on short breaks like this, I sometimes forget to even call—I'm having too much fun.

After I'd shut my phone and put it into my pocket, I went to explain the traffic problem we'd had to Winnie, and to ask about the unexpected crowds in

5

town. She seemed flustered, though. Stressed. And I couldn't help but wonder if somehow our visit, though expected, was ill timed.

"I could scare up some coffee and sandwiches for you now, if you're hungry," she offered. "Though it might be better to get settled into your digs first. Can you hold off until dinner? I've reserved a table here for the three of you for the late seating—'late' meaning eightish.

"Sorry I can't put you up myself," she explained, "but my apartment above the restaurant is small, and I haven't got a spare room. Fortunately, I made reservations a month ago for you at the Under Mountain Inn—before the crowds hit. The inn's old, but modernized, so you'll be comfortable. It's within walking distance from here and all the shopping."

George put her hand on Winnie's shoulder. "Hey, whatever! I'm sure the inn's great. But why all the tourists? Isn't it off-season?"

Winnie made a face and dropped her voice. "I *should* be grateful. We need the business around here after the past two years. There's been no snow . . . and it's been too warm for the snowmaking machinery to work well. Ski season's been a total loss, and then this year, with the summer drought followed by all that October rain, leaf season was a disaster. The whole area is depressed."

"It sure doesn't look it now." I motioned to outside the bay window. People strolled down the sidewalks, dipping into stores. The cars were moving at a crawl.

"Exactly. Which is why I *should* be happy." Winnie shrugged. "And I am . . . at least financially. I can barely keep up with the business. But it's too much. And with the TV crew, the media, and the increased police presence, Brody's Junction feels more like Boston than home these days."

"TV crew?" Bess repeated, and moved closer to the window. "Is some new show set here?"

Mary Beth looked up from setting a table and giggled. "You're kidding, right? Like, you haven't a clue?"

For a moment Winnie looked at George, puzzled, then threw her hands up. "Of course. Why should you girls know what's going on here? I guess the news hadn't hit River Heights before you left town."

"What news?" George asked, sounding as impatient as I felt.

Joel made a spooky theatrical sound, then grinned sheepishly as Winnie warned him off with a hard look. "They aren't from around here, Joel." She turned back toward us. "It seems we've been invaded not just by tourists—but by aliens."

2

Reel TV

Aliens?" **I wasn't sure** I'd heard right.

"As in people from other countries?" George suggested.

Joel jumped right in. "Nope." He looked gleeful. "More like creatures from another *planet*."

"As in UFOs?" George looked dubious.

"As in UFOs," Winnie repeated, sounding a little flat. For some reason she didn't seem to share Joel's enthusiasm for their extraterrestrial visitors.

"Right!" Bess caught my eye. Her expression mirrored my own skepticism. "Aliens, like in the movies."

I waited for Winnie to start laughing.

She didn't.

"You're kidding, right?" This had to be some kind of joke.

She shook her head. "It isn't. Not that *I'm* convinced they're real," she added quickly. "But lots of people are buying into it." She motioned out the window. A white van with a national cable network logo was stopped at the light. It sported a satellite antenna on top.

"The media sure *hope* the UFOs are the real deal," Joel pointed out.

Just then, someone called from the kitchen. "Scarletti, get in here. . . . Something's weird with this sauce."

"Duty calls. Be right there," Joel shouted back. "See you guys," he said, as he disappeared into the back of the restaurant.

Winnie let out a tired sigh. "And *that's* the problem. . . . Everyone is so distracted and excited by all the craziness—TV crews, crowds, reporters—they're making mistakes." She gave a meaningful glance to Mary Beth, the waiter, who was still setting up for dinner. "My waiters are constantly poking their heads outside to check the sky for spaceships. The one saving grace is that the customers are equally distracted. But in the long run I'm wondering if these UFOs are going to hurt the dinner trade."

"The aliens turn up at dinnertime?" George said with a straight face.

Winnie cracked a smile. "Seems that way. They favor nighttime. Though I recall there was at least one daytime sighting."

Why mainly at night? I wondered, as George spoke up. "Looks to me like your visitors from outer space have put Brody's Junction on the map."

"UFOs in Vermont?" Bess started to giggle. "It's too much. Little green men, deciding to land in the Green Mountain State!"

"Maybe they're little red men wearing green snowsuits," George suggested.

"Martian fashionistas!" I laughed.

"Laugh if you want," Mary Beth said, looking up from behind the counter. She had picked up a fresh supply of napkins. The real fear in her voice wiped the smile right off my face. "But the state police, the sheriff, the mayor, and the crew of a reality TV show are taking them seriously. Even the FBI has sent investigators."

"The FBI?" Maybe this *was* a bigger deal than we were making it out to be.

"Yes, even the FBI," Winnie said, then turned to give some instructions to Mary Beth.

The possibility of UFOs and all the publicity surrounding sightings explained away the mystery of the traffic and the increased police presence in the small town. "How come it's not on the national news?" I asked.

Winnie shrugged. "The first sightings didn't cause much of a stir. Most folks around here thought the kids reporting seeing UFOs on a Friday night had either been partying too hard or were playing pranks. Even when they had pictures."

"There are *pictures*?" Bess looked interested.

"Computer generated," George predicted. "Altered through a photo program."

"No one's been able to tell either way, though the FBI took the photos with them for forensic studies."

"Which proved what?" I asked.

"Nothing yet," Winnie answered. "Or at least no one is talking about what they might have found. But there are experts from NASA in town, plus all this press—which leads me to think they probably turned up something. The national media will be broadcasting this news this weekend, for sure. Joel tells me the latest local blogs are full of the reports. I'm surprised you didn't come across them, George," Winnie said.

George's reputation as a technophile preceded her. She shrugged. "I saw some stuff, but didn't bother to read it. Nuts are constantly reporting alien sightings online. I ignore them."

"Is this the first time national TV networks have bothered to send reporters?" I asked, looking out the window as the cable network's van made a left at the corner. Watching it made my spirits sink. Who wanted to spend a vacation in the middle of some crazy media circus? Then again . . . there could be a real mystery here.

Winnie nodded. "Makes it all seem more real."

George turned toward Winnie. "Tell me, you don't really believe in UFOs, do you? Have you ever seen them yourself?"

"Yes," Winnie said. "Twice. But," she added pointedly, "that doesn't mean they're the real thing. Half the troopers are convinced they're hoaxes. But once the *Reel TV* crew airs its footage next week, half the UFO fanatics in the country are going to invade this town big-time."

I had watched *Reel TV*'s reality show once or twice. Personally I couldn't believe anyone was taken in by their investigations of paranormal situations. "So that explains all the 'No Vacancy' signs on the motels and inns on the way here," I remarked.

"I wish I'd bothered to read the online reports. Maybe I will now." George walked over to Winnie's laptop open on the counter. "Can I log on now? My computer's still back in the car."

"You can't. My system keeps crashing. Maybe you can find the problem. Everything's affected: my e-mail, my address book, my website, and today I couldn't even access any of my bookkeeping programs."

George peeled off her down vest. "Maybe it's a virus. Let me check it out."

Winnie stopped her. "Not now, George. I've got to get into the kitchen and deal with dinner, and you guys must want to settle in after your trip. My friend

Sarah Conway, the owner of Under Mountain Inn, called. She's holding your room. Given the crush of tourists, you'd better check in now. You'll like Sarah. She'll make you feel right at home."

"Okay," George said. "I'll run some diagnostics on your system after dinner, if you feel it can wait. We can catch up on family news then—Mom's dying to know what's new with you and the café."

Under Mountain Inn was all that Winnie had promised, and I was secretly pleased that she had lacked the room to put us up herself.

The three-story white building had several gables with steeply sloped black slate roofs. Green shutters framed the windows. Several hearty souls were parked on wicker benches on the wraparound porch, watching the sun slide down behind the low hills to the west of town. In the fading afternoon light a single electric candle burned in every window, giving the establishment a cozy, welcoming look. An inscription over the front door said the original inn, parts of which were still standing, dated from 1801.

I couldn't help but think that if the place hadn't looked so well-kept and freshly painted, it would have been the perfect setting for a ghost story. Old-fashioned and creepy. Instead, though, it was modernized, refreshed—and beautiful.

When we arrived, a woman was on the phone behind the reception desk. While we waited to register, I looked around. The lobby was spacious and welcoming. It flowed into a large, comfortable lounge generously furnished with an assortment of couches and overstuffed easy chairs. A cozy fire burned in the fireplace, and at the far end of the room an archway opened into a dining room.

As soon as she hung up the phone, the woman introduced herself as Sarah Conway, the innkeeper. When we mentioned we were Winnie's guests, she hurried out from behind the desk and warmly pumped our hands. "Winnie told me all about you girls." Turning toward George, she said, "I know you from the pictures of you and your mom that Winnie has up in her apartment. One of you is Bess, and the other is Nancy—the amateur detective!" She looked from me to Bess and back at me again. "You're Nancy, right? And you"—she looked at Bess—"must be Bess."

"I'm impressed." I laughed. "How did you know?"

Sarah blushed. "I've seen Bess's picture too—after all, she's George's cousin, and there are photos from that family reunion a few years back."

After calling for someone to cover the desk, Sarah personally escorted us to the third floor. She was open-faced and talkative, and seemed determined to give us special treatment because we were Winnie's friends. "I hate putting you all into such cramped quarters," she apologized as she climbed the stairs ahead of us.

Our room was at one end of the long hall. "At least you get a view of the mountain." She unlocked the door. "I put you guys in the best room I could spare up here. The other two are rented out to the TV crew. They haven't got the view."

True to her word, the room was barely large enough for three twin beds and one rocking chair. A large old-fashioned wardrobe stood next to a dresser. Tieback curtains framed each of the two windows: One provided a view of the mountain, and the other opened onto a fire escape.

"Winnie probably told you about the tourist invasion. Not that anyone in town is complaining," Sarah told us.

George looked up from rummaging in her duffle bag. "Mom had mentioned that Winnie was having second thoughts about refinancing the café because things were so slow. We were amazed to see everything booming." While George talked, she stowed her computer and backpack on top of the wardrobe. She deposited her running gear onto the bed. Earlier she had announced we were all in dire need of a good run—particularly after sitting so long all day, and with the prospect of a gourmet calorie-laden dinner facing us that evening.

While we unpacked, Sarah continued to talk. "The UFO sightings took everyone by surprise. Most tradesmen and merchants are pretty happy about it. It's hard for the restaurants to handle the crowds, though. Take Winnie's place, for instance. It's all too much to deal with on top of her other problems." Abruptly she stopped and checked her watch. "But don't get me started about Winnie and her life. Likely you're more in the know than I am," she said to George. "I've got to get downstairs, pronto. The TV crew pulled in just before you girls. The producer was pretty miffed they couldn't have the whole place to themselves—offered me good money too, but I'm not going to turn down the few regulars I have this time of year to put those people up! The minute some hot new story breaks, they'll drop the UFO angle and be gone. Fat lot of good that'll do me next year." With that, she hurried out the door.

I waited until I heard her footsteps fade down the hall. "Is Winnie in some kind of trouble?" I asked George.

"Other than slow business, nothing I've heard about." As George changed into her sweats, she added, "Mom would have mentioned anything serious—I think." However, George appeared worried as she stuffed her duffle under the bed.

Bess tried to reassure George. "You're right. If Winnie's problems were superserious, your mom would have told you." As she put on a vintage River Heights High letter jacket, she added, "More to the point, Winnie would have asked us to postpone this trip."

"Bess is right," I said. "Unless, of course, Winnie never told her something was wrong—or something cropped up after we left."

"Maybe Mom just didn't feel free to share all of Winnie's problems with me," George said. "Whatever—I'm glad we're here. Maybe we can help her out." George put one foot up on the dresser and began doing her pre-workout stretches.

"Good thinking," I added. "As soon as I've worked out and before we come back to change for dinner, I'm going to corner Sarah and find out what she didn't tell us."

Bess laughed. "That won't take much prodding. She looked ready to burst out every detail . . . until she realized how late it was. Which reminds me, we'd better go running now, or we'll be late for dinner."

Bess had a point. Frankly, I was ready to skip the run. Sarah's comments had stirred my curiosity. It sounded like Winnie was in trouble—and I was confused about why George had had no idea at all.

As we headed out for our run, we saw the inn's staff gathering luggage from the reception area and carting it upstairs. Members of the *Reel TV* crew—the name was on their jackets and sweatshirts—were sorting shiny metal film canisters and camera equipment. The crew milled around the front desk as Sarah registered the new arrivals.

She waved as we passed. "Have a good run," she called out. She started to say something else, but a siren's wail drowned out her next words.

"Sounds like a fire somewhere," I said, hurrying over toward the porch. The door flew open in my face, and a dark-haired man stepped through the entrance, blocking my exit. He was only a little taller than me.

He swept a shock of straight black hair back from his forehead, and he shouted, "Izzy, they're back." Without waiting for a response, he raced back out. I followed him. I watched from the porch steps as he tore over to a white van idling by the curb. He threw open the back doors.

Before I could see what he was unloading, Bess and George hurried out onto the porch. "What's going on?"

"I'm not sure," I answered. People were pouring

out of shops, restaurants, and houses, streaming toward the town square. "Maybe there's a fire somewhere."

"No," Sarah cried. "Like he said, they're back." She grabbed my arm and half pulled me along with her. "Come on, girls," she shouted to Bess and George. "If it's anything like last time, you'll get a better view from the square."

The town square was packed, and we were relegated to the back of the crowd. All heads were turned skyward. Sarah pointed toward the east over the mountain. Circles of light revolved slowly against the deepening blue sky. They hung, suspended, over the meadow for a moment. Then they swept the circumference of the field and hovered.

The effect was hypnotic.

"This is totally unreal," I murmured. It had to be a hoax. Right?

3

Skywatch

In spite of myself I was spellbound. I gaped as the revolving spheres of light descended in lazy circles over the meadow. Though they were bright, their eerie glow barely lit the ground, and I wondered why.

Whatever those lights were, I could *not* believe they were spaceships. But why didn't they make any noise? These didn't look in the least like gliders—how could they fly without engines? There was absolutely no sound, though. The objects floated across the sky in complete silence.

The same silence seemed to have smothered the excited chatter of the crowd. I shifted my gaze away from the sky and glanced around. All eyes were turned up.

The eerie quiet sent a chill up my spine.

Somewhere behind me and to my left, a camera whirred. Someone was filming the event.

As I checked to see who, a gasp went up from the crowd. I quickly looked back up at the sky, just in time to see the flying objects change course. First they spiraled sharply upward, and then, with no warning, they vanished in a blinding flash of light, leaving only the stars and constellations twinkling overhead.

Instantly the spell was broken. The town square erupted in cries and comments and exclamations. Everyone began talking all at once.

"Why are they here?" one voice said.

"No good reason, I'll tell you that."

"Don't jump to conclusions," someone contradicted. "They've been quiet and peaceful. They haven't threatened us."

"They will," another person responded. "They will. And the government knows all about it—why else would the Feds be here?"

I couldn't believe what I was hearing. Apparently no one doubted the UFOs were real. No one but me, it seemed.

Bess shook my arm. She looked incredulous. "Tell me you saw what I just saw."

"I saw *something*," I answered. There had to be some sort of rational explanation for what had just happened over that mountain.

"So I wasn't imagining things." Bess dug her fists deep into her jacket.

"If you were, so was everyone else," George broke in. "Pretty convincing special effects," she suggested.

"But how?" I asked.

"Beats me," George said. "At least it's caught on tape! That guy we saw at the hotel, the one who tipped us off about this, was right behind me. He filmed the whole thing."

"Oh, right," Sarah said, shivering in the cold. "That was the cameraman from the *Reel TV* crew. Pretty amazing, those folk turning up just in time for a sighting."

"They're staying at your inn, aren't they?" another woman asked Sarah. Sarah told her yes, most of them. The two women then began discussing the sighting, as the crowd continued to disperse.

Most of the spectators were heading back to cars, or to shops and restaurants. A few groups, including some state troopers, hung back, milling around the square. A couple of patrol cars, lights flashing, sirens blasting, raced down the road leading east. I figured they were going to the area of the sighting. I wished I was going with them. I wanted to take a firsthand look at that meadow, check out the ground for evidence—not that I could see much in the dark. I found it hard to believe these UFOs were real.

Apparently, so did George.

"I wish I had my camera," George grumbled. "There was something fishy about those UFOs."

"I didn't notice anyone taking pictures," I admitted. "Just that one guy from the TV show. Though I'm sure other people taped the event." It was hard to imagine tourists without cameras and camcorders.

"Even if people did film the sighting, I wouldn't have noticed," Bess said. "I was afraid to look away from the sky in case when I looked back, the UFOs would be gone."

I had felt something similar—as if I was compelled to look. What troubled me most was their silence. "Did you notice they made no noise?"

"They never do." A smug voice announced from behind me.

I turned to face a thin bearded man. He was about five-foot-ten and had glasses mended with a piece of adhesive tape across the nosepiece. Decidedly dorky, he was probably twentysomething, but he was already balding, and his circle of stringy blond hair hung down almost to his shoulders. His clothes looked seriously thrift store, but they were clean.

He smiled at me. His straight white teeth were at odds with his wardrobe and his straggly beard. I found his smile unnerving, and his smug tone bordered on offensive.

Before I could say anything, he added, "They are almost always quiet as death. At least in published accounts."

Bess leapt into the conversation. "You've read a lot about UFOs?" she asked. Unlike me, she didn't seem to be put off by his tone—though I could well imagine what she thought of his taste in clothes.

He gave a tight laugh. "Sure. I write about them too. Is this your first sighting?"

"Yes," George volunteered, but her cautious expression matched my own. "Not that I'm convinced that what we saw was the real thing."

"But everyone seemed to have seen it," Bess broke in.

"Oh, it was real enough," I said. "The question is, how did they do it?"

"They?" The bearded man tilted his head and studied me. I admit, I found his scrutiny unsettling. "Exactly who might *'they'* be?"

"You tell me," I shot back, then winced at the tone of my own voice. I tried to soften my response. "You've seen them before—or at least, I got that impression."

"Not often." He smiled a thin-lipped smile, then lifted both his shoulders. "Only here," he added.

"You think they're real?" Bess wanted to know.

He shrugged again. "I don't know. I'm not sure. Some folks do."

"Have any of these sightings ever been proven valid?" I asked.

"Depends who you talk to, and what you mean by proof." He gestured vaguely around at the quickly dispersing crowd. "Most of these people want the UFOs to be real. I'm open to it, either way. The press here wants it to be the real thing . . . and so, in a way, do I." With that, he walked off.

"That man is seriously scuzzy," Bess remarked. It was obvious the man's sloppy dress and bad grooming offended Bess's fashion sense. But something else about him made me vaguely uneasy.

"He positively reeks of geek!" George added. "I predict he's a serious techy. And he doesn't sound like he's from around here."

"He's not." Sarah's friends had left, and apparently she'd overheard George's comment. "He's from Boston. He's a journalist and a science fiction writer, though no one around here has heard of him. He's renting one of Addie May and Aldwin Nichols's cabins at an off-season rate. He's up this way every year. Name's Nathan Blackman. Gives me the creeps, that's what he does."

Sarah headed back toward the inn. We decided to

take a short run, then we returned to our room.

Since Bess had first dibs on the shower, I decided to learn more about UFOs—particularly about these recent local sightings. "Can we check out UFOs on your laptop?"

"Great minds think alike," George responded. She took the laptop from the top of the wardrobe, then sat cross-legged on the bed and booted up the computer. "Gives me a chance to check out the wi-fi connection here at the inn."

"They have wireless in a place this old?" Bess remarked as George quickly went online.

I picked up one of the brochures from the dresser and showed it to Bess. "Sarah's a good businesswoman. Apparently she's upgraded everything from the heating system to phone lines to wi-fi—but she's kept the traditional old New England look. That's a big selling point for this place."

"Let me know what you dig up on UFOs," Bess said as she headed for her shower.

Meanwhile, George had googled up a slew of UFO sites.

I sat next to her on the bed. A zillion or so Web pages were devoted to extraterrestrials, crop circles, and close encounters of every possible kind. "Why am I not surprised?" I said. "Maybe we should refine the search." I thought a moment. "Add *hoaxes.*"

George obliged, with a warning. "That's ruling out right from the get-go the possibility that UFOs might be the real thing."

"Don't tell me you believe . . . ," I started to protest, then caught the twinkle in George's big brown eyes. I punched her shoulder lightly. "You had me there for a minute."

George's expression shifted slightly. Her tone was almost wistful as she said, "I'm afraid part of me, like that guy Nathan at the square, wishes they were real. Can you imagine the technology a species advanced enough to send visitors here might have?"

Honestly I couldn't, but I was sure tech-savvy George could.

While she talked, she surfed to a couple of sites, then finally stopped on one. "This looks promising," she said. It belonged to an organization that investigated paranormal activities. "They don't sound as negative as the others. I don't know about you, Nancy, but I'm not interested in the theories of people who just dismiss this stuff. Whoever is perpetrating these hoaxes is pretty clever . . . and there's always the possibility that some sightings are real."

When Bess came out of the bathroom, George handed me the laptop before washing for dinner. While Bess phoned home on her cell, I read up on UFOs. By the time it was my turn to freshen up, I was somewhat surprised and thoroughly confused.

Even planetarium websites admitted that most, but not all, UFO sightings could be explained away as either hoaxes or honest mistakes.

I took the little notebook I always carry out of my purse and listed some of the honest mistakes made by witnesses. Spectators sometimes mistook ordinary aircraft for UFOs because of a trick of light or the angle of the sun or moon. Weather balloons were another culprit. Most nations' militaries would never admit the existence of spy balloons, but even the famous sighting in Roswell, New Mexico, during the 1940s was possibly due to a spy balloon the government refused to admit existed.

I listed more possibilities and made a note to check out some online weather information sites later. It seemed that sometimes weather phenomena could trick the eye, often at sunset or twilight, or even on a cloudy night.

As we headed downstairs, I shared my findings with Bess and George. We were still talking about the sighting when we walked through the lobby. The *Reel TV* crew was enjoying hors d'oeuvres and cocktails in the lounge before heading into the dining room for dinner. I spied the crew's cameraman on the far side of the lounge, and made a mental note to try to speak to him about the footage he'd shot during the sighting. I wondered if I could convince him to let me see it.

"What surprises me," Bess admitted as we threaded our way through the knot of people clustered near an hors d'oeuvres tray on the reception desk, "is that all the sightings *aren't* proven to be hoaxes. It's not reasonable, though, to think that anyone—or any*thing*—smart enough to build spacecraft powerful enough to travel for light-years to get here would bother hovering over mountains in Vermont, or New Mexico, for that matter."

"My feelings exactly," I said as we were passing the reception desk. "It just doesn't make sense."

"Does everything have to make sense?" A woman leaning against the reception desk asked me. She shifted her glass of wine from her right hand to her left and introduced herself. "I know it's rude to eavesdrop, but I'm a producer at *Reel TV*, and I couldn't help but overhear you. My name's Isabel Sanchez—people call me Izzy. And you're . . . ?"

"Nancy Drew," I answered, shaking her hand. Her grip was firm and strong. Isabel Sanchez looked to be barely thirty, and radiated pure energy. I found myself instantly liking her, in spite of her seeming overly nosy and very aggressive. I introduced George and Bess.

"Anyway," she continued, focusing her large dark eyes on me. "I couldn't help but overhear what you said. I'm not sure I agree." She interrupted herself with a throaty laugh. She had a warm, deep voice and talked at the speed of light. "You see, I produce all the *Reel TV* episodes—and what *doesn't* make sense is what the show is all about. You know, ghost sightings, haunted houses, out-of-body experiences, and now aliens among us. That's why we came to Brody's Junction."

"To film UFOs," I stated. Could this be my opening to ask to see some footage? Before I could ask, Izzy shook her head.

"No—well, yes *and* no. Of course we want to film the UFOs. That's half of our program—presenting weird phenomena and letting our audience judge how real or unreal they might be. But the other half is to see how people—people like you girls—react to the paranormal."

"Or faked alien sightings," George added.

"You're sure they're fake?" Izzy challenged.

"Are they ever real?" I shot back.

Izzy shrugged. "I don't know. But what I know or think isn't the point. The point is I'd love to have permission to follow you girls around and get your reaction to the goings-on in town. To make you part of our show. We'd pay you, of course."

Bess's eyes widened. "We'd be on television? Hey, I'm game."

"Count me out," George replied instantly.

"Why us?" I asked. I found her request off-putting, though I wasn't sure why. "Why not ask some other tourists to be on your show?"

"Because you're not believers. I know you're not, Nancy, and I'm assuming you two," she said, looking at Bess and George, "aren't either. I want to record your reactions to what's happening in this town. The change from doubt to belief when you finally see that the UFOs are legit."

"And you're sure they are?" I shot back.

"I'm open to the possibility," Izzy answered. "By the way, I'm in room 302, in case you decide to join us. Or leave a note for me at the desk."

4

Sabotage

"So the big-time producer's your neighbor," Winnie remarked to us over coffee and pumpkin pie. The café was slowly emptying out, and the last guests were finishing up their desserts. Taking advantage of the slowdown, Winnie had poured herself a cup of coffee, then joined us at our table.

"Right, we're in room 301," I said. "The *Reel TV* producer is in 302."

"Convenient, in case we decide to bang on her door in the middle of the night and accept her offer to have our every step shadowed by her camera crew," George remarked wryly.

"It might have been fun, being on TV and all," Bess said, spooning another dollop of whipped cream onto her pie.

"I'm glad you opted out," Winnie said. "Not that I have anything against Ms. Sanchez personally. I met her earlier this month when she came to scout locations in town. She was nice enough, but I felt like the vultures were descending. Maybe that's too strong a word." Winnie ran her finger around the edge of her cup. "But between us, I much preferred Brody's Junction when the media hadn't heard of us, and the town was just a blip on the ski radar."

"And not on whatever passes for radar on a UFO," George joked.

"Right!" Winnie slapped the table and chuckled. "I knew it was a good idea to have you guys visit. I haven't had a good laugh in weeks," she said.

I waited for her to explain why she needed us around to share a laugh. But a couple motioned for their check, and Winnie was instantly on her feet. "Let me take care of these people. I'll be right back."

While Winnie tended to her customers, I glanced at the wall behind Bess's head. A framed photo caught my eye.

In it, Winnie and another woman were standing in front of the café, arms slung around each other's shoulders. They both wore goofy chef's hats and aprons and were grinning like schoolgirls in a high school yearbook. Below the photo was a smaller frame. Inside the frame was a shabby dollar bill. I figured it was a good luck souvenir—the first dollar the restaurant had earned.

Bess turned to see what I was staring at. "Who's that with Winnie?" she asked George.

George took a closer look. "It must be Winnie's original business partner. She opened the café with a cousin who's also a food person. I don't know her name, but she's no longer part of the business."

"What happened?" I wondered.

"I don't know," George answered. "I'm not even sure my mother knows the details."

"I read somewhere that business partnerships break up all the time," Bess said.

Up front Winnie was putting some pastries into a box. The long front counter served as a display case for the café's take-out baked goods. The cash register, Winnie's laptop, and a small display of local tourist brochures were at the far end of the counter.

While I was watching, Winnie rang up the sale, said good-bye to her guests, and noted something in an accounting book next to the cash register. Winnie seemed like such an open, pleasant person, I found it hard to believe she'd have problems with a business partner. She started keying something into the computer. Then she frowned, jiggled the mouse, and poked some keys a few times. "Not again!" she said, pounding her fist on the counter.

She turned toward our table. "George. The whole system just crashed—for the *third time* today!" She sounded on the verge of tossing the whole machine out the café window.

"Not to worry!" George hurried over to the counter. Bess and I followed.

As I leaned over the counter to watch George, I knocked a loose-leaf book off the counter. "Sorry!" I bent to pick it up. The rings inside the binder had snapped open, and a few sheets had fallen out. As I reinserted them into the binder, I saw they were recipes: some neatly typed, others handwritten on paper yellowing with age.

I handed the book back to Winnie. "It's okay, Nancy," she said. She put the book on a shelf behind the counter. "I shouldn't have left it there. Any chance I get, I'm trying to enter my recipes onto the computer." She shook her head in dismay. "Probably all of the info I put in today—bookkeeping, recipes, whatever—is lost. I hadn't backed it up yet."

"You're in luck. George can retrieve almost anything," Bess said.

"If I can get it up and running." George was half talking to herself as she tried to get the blank screen to come to life.

"Is it serious?" I asked, peering over George's shoulder at the screen.

George didn't answer. She continued to press a few keys. Suddenly the screen flickered to life.

"All right!" George started to smile, then she groaned as the screen filled with rows of gibberish and nonsense characters. A moment later a leering animated cartoon face appeared on the screen and let out a mocking laugh.

"What's that?" Winnie asked.

"I have no idea," George said. "But one thing's for sure. Someone's hacked into your system big-time."

A Tempting Offer

Hacked in?" **Winnie pulled** up a stool and sat down heavily.

"Who would do this to you?" Bess asked.

"And why?" I wondered.

George tapped on some keys while thinking out loud. "This looks like a pretty sophisticated job," she said.

"So you can't fix it?" Winnie seemed close to tears.

"I didn't say that." George kept her focus on the screen. "It'll just take some time." She kept drumming her fingers on the keyboard, thinking. "Here's a thought. Maybe we're jumping to conclusions. Maybe the hacking isn't just aimed at Winnie's machine."

"Maybe it's some kind of glitch caused by the UFOs—or *whatever* they are," Bess said.

37

"Or someone playing a prank—knowing half the town would suspect UFOs were behind any tech breakdown," I suggested.

"I'll check it out," George said, retrieving her backpack from our table. She took out her laptop and switched it on. It booted right up. George tested a couple of programs, went online, then looked up from her screen. "It's fine. The problem's limited to your system after all," she told Winnie.

"It figures." Winnie blew out her breath. "The way everything's been going lately around here, I'm beginning to feel jinxed."

"Jinxed?" I repeated. My mind catapulted back to Sarah Conway's mention of Winnie's troubles.

Winnie gave an embarrassed laugh. "There are probably reasonable explanations . . ."

"For . . . ?" George said, encouraging her.

"Lots of little problems have been cropping up at the café," Winnie explained. "I'm not even sure they're connected. The ovens broke down last week, and somehow the baking powder and flour containers got mislabeled, and we had to throw out a whole evening's baking. Just yesterday the plug on the cappuccino machine fell off. Joel had to take it to be repaired—I won't have it back until tomorrow, and we're so busy."

As I listened, I felt as if I were looking at a puzzle where the dots didn't really connect—and yet my sixth sense, known for helping me solve tough mysteries, told me otherwise. "Do you have any explanation?" I asked.

"In my saner moments," she answered, "I chalk it up to being understaffed and overbusy. I've been through this kind of stress before. You start making mistakes in the kitchen—everything from not-so-minor accidents, like cutting yourself during prep or burning your hand on a hot pot, to dumb things, like going to drain pasta in the sink and forgetting the colander." Again, Winnie looked sheepish.

"And when you're feeling not so sane?" Bess asked. Her tone was light, but the question was reasonable. I'd been wondering the same thing.

Winnie colored slightly. "Oh, I think someone is deliberately sabotaging me and the restaurant."

Sabotage? Before I could ask her who or why, Winnie gave a dismissive wave of her hand.

"Like I said, I'm probably blowing things out of proportion . . ." As I watched, her expression shifted from embarrassed to puzzled to something I couldn't quite read. "It can't be." She seemed to be figuring something out—out loud. "Hacking into a computer—how would she?—I can't believe . . ." Winnie's words trailed off as the door to the kitchen swung open.

Joel emerged. He wore a beat-up shearling jacket

over his apron and thick winter gloves on his hands. "Boss, we've got a problem."

Winnie's jaw dropped.

"It's the freezer again. The back section is fine, but the front is defrosting at a pretty scary rate, and we just got that meat order in this morning."

"The freezer." To my amazement, Winnie sounded relieved. "That's all?" She turned to George. "This is an ongoing problem I've had since the café opened. The new freezer's on order, but meanwhile, I've got to deal with this." She headed for the kitchen.

"What about the computer?" George asked.

Winnie stopped and turned. "Do you need me, or can you just deal with it?"

"No problemo!" George waved her off. "Go ahead—I'll have it up and running before we leave." Immediately she sat down at the computer. Bess and I exchanged a glance, and knew it was time to leave George to wrestle with the computer.

Winnie told us to help ourselves to more coffee and dessert, then followed Joel into the kitchen.

As the doors closed behind Winnie, Bess lowered her voice and said, "I wonder who 'she' is?"

"Whoever this mystery woman may be, Winnie doesn't think she has the tech skills to hack into her system." A pot of hot water was on the coffee machine heater. I located a tin of tea bags and made myself a cup of tea. As it brewed, I mentally reviewed the list of Winnie's mishaps. At first glance all the incidents seemed like just a run of bad luck. But what if Winnie was right, and someone *was* sabotaging her?

Within the hour George had Winnie's system up and running. "I need to come back tomorrow morning to install a better firewall," she reported. "I'll ask Winnie to stay offline until then."

After saying good night, we headed back to the inn. When we arrived, Sarah invited us into the lounge. A meeting with the mayor, some town officials, the police, and the *Reel TV* people had just broken up. "You all look a bit chilled," she said. "Why not help yourselves to hot chocolate and something sweet?"

Bess patted her stomach. "We've all had more than our share of dessert, but something hot sounds great. It's getting cold out there."

Sarah smiled broadly as we took off our jackets. "Snow's predicted any day now. Maybe our spell of dry, warm winters is about to break."

"Let me get rid of my backpack," George said, then ran upstairs to our room, taking our jackets with her.

I followed Sarah into the lounge. This was the perfect chance to track down the cameraman who had filmed the UFO sighting. After a cursory glance at the crowd I asked Sarah if he was still there, or if he'd already gone to his room.

Sarah looked up from filling a mug with hot chocolate. "Oh, you mean Frankie Lee. He's not staying at the inn. Ms. Sanchez rented a house for him up the road a ways. His family's flying in from the West Coast next week to spend some time here, and we just didn't have room." She handed me the drink. "He should still be around, though. I overheard him say he had to speak with Ms. Sanchez about some production notes."

"I'd like to meet him," I said.

"I'd be happy to do the honors," she said, but we hadn't moved two steps away from the buffet when a spare, rangy man stopped us. "Who's your friend?" he asked Sarah. He was over six feet tall, and he looked like he was in his seventies. His sandy hair was faded and thinning; his face was narrow. But his pale blue eyes shone sharp as a hawk's. He smiled and reached out to shake my hand even before we were introduced.

"Oh, Ethan, this is Nancy Drew. She and her friends are visiting Winifred. And, young as she is, she's a bona fide detective."

I was dismayed at that introduction—I like to keep my sleuthing private when I can, just in case it gets in the way of my getting some evidence. Ethan lifted his eyebrows. "Impressive," he said.

"And Nancy, this is Ethan Brody. He's the mayor of Brody's Junction."

"Who's a detective?" a shorter, beefy man inquired

as he walked up. He wore a state trooper uniform and held a cup of coffee in one hand.

"Nancy here is," Sarah said. Then she introduced me. "This is Captain Rupert Greene. Rupert's stationed at the barracks just outside of town."

Captain Greene seemed to appraise me carefully as he shook my hand. "Someone called you in to investigate?"

"I'm just here visiting friends," I told him.

He nodded, but I sensed he didn't believe me.

Mayor Brody chuckled. "Rupert, don't look so suspicious. A detective on the case might be just what we need." From his tone I couldn't tell if the mayor was mocking me. Not that I wasn't used to officials being skeptical. After all, teenagers aren't usually known for investigating crimes. Speaking of crimes, though—I wondered if these guys were talking about the UFO sightings.

"What's there to investigate?" I was sure I knew the answer, but figured playing a bit dumb wasn't a bad idea here.

"Alien invaders!" the captain said, grinning from ear to ear.

The mayor patted the captain on the shoulder. "Our lawman here likes to joke about our small town being on the front lines of an intergalactic war zone," he said with a disarming smile. "But don't let his joshing fool you. He's taking it seriously enough to cordon off the perimeter of the sightings."

Captain Greene let out a hearty laugh. "Ethan's right. I'm pretty skeptical they're the real thing." Then he asked, "Were you around earlier this evening?"

"Yes."

"So what's your take on our otherworldy visitors?" His tone was serious, but the shadow of a smile played across his lips.

I saw I had an ally. The state police captain believed the UFOs were about as real as the man in the moon. "That they have more to do with *this* world than the stars," I answered. I wondered if I could convince him to give me access to the area where the UFOs had appeared.

Mayor Brody's eyebrows shot up even higher. "You've found yourself another skeptic, Rupert." He turned to me. "You think our UFO sightings are hoaxes, then?"

Our sightings. That was a strange way of putting it. But I attributed his remark to hometown pride. "Probably," I answered.

"Which is why," Izzy Sanchez said as she joined us, "I want to use Nancy and her friends in our documentary."

Captain Greene practically choked on his coffee. "To prove the UFOs don't exist?" he asked the TV producer.

"Actually, just the opposite," Izzy said. She smiled

44

at me. "I confess, I'm an incurable eavesdropper, so I couldn't help but overhear that you are some kind of detective?"

Mayor Brody answered for me. "She is."

"*Amateur* detective," I pointed out. I was trying to maintain a guise of not having much experience, in case it ruffled anyone—but at the rate news was spreading about my sleuthing rep, I feared it was a lost cause.

"So much the better," Izzy said. "That's the perfect touch. The camera will record your efforts to prove that the sightings are a hoax. The drama will be even more intense when the viewers realize, at the same time as you, that they aren't. The detective bit gives more weight to the whole thing."

"Like I said before, I'm not interested." I turned to ask Captain Greene about visiting the site, but he was already talking with someone else.

"What can I do to convince you?" Izzy asked. I must say, I admired her persistence. It sure piqued my curiosity.

"Why me and my friends, again?"

"Like I told you earlier: You girls are young enough to appeal to our target audience; they'll identify with you. The three of you will look good on-screen . . ."

I finished her sentence for her. "And of course, there will be more drama when you convince me these hoaxes are real. But what if I don't get convinced?"

She wasn't about to give up. "If you worked with us, you could move freely around some of the restricted areas—at least while the crew is around."

The woman was as dogged as I was. "You sure know how to play a person."

"That's a big part of my job—convincing people to do something they *think* they don't want to do." She paused. I could tell she was waiting for my reply. I wanted to say no, but my need to get to the root of this mystery was too strong. The UFOs were a hoax, and in spite of what Izzy might think, I was going to prove it.

"So?" she asked.

"Okay, okay, you got me. I'm game. I can't speak for George or Bess, though—we're here together on vacation. If they don't want to go ahead with the deal, then it's off." Of course, I knew Bess would jump at the chance to be on TV, and George would go along with the whole thing, if only because she was always a good sport in the end.

"All right!" Izzy pumped her fist in the air. A second later she was all business. "I'll have one of my people leave releases for you to sign in the morning. Part of my crew will be at the roadblock at the foot of the hill leading up to Brody's Peak Resort. You can hook up with one of the camera teams there before lunch, if possible. It'll give you a chance to get closer to the scene of your so-called crime."

6

Booted Out

I **'m sure the TV** crew won't bother with me," George said the next morning after breakfast at the inn. When she looked up from signing her copy of the release Izzy's people had left at the reception desk, relief was written on her face.

"True," Bess said, zipping up her fleece jacket. "Watching you fine-tune Winnie's computer isn't exactly the stuff of exciting television."

"Ah, but taping you shop—now that could make for some pretty hot TV drama," George told her as we headed for the parking lot.

"We're going shopping?" I asked, looking at Bess.

She brandished a Brody's Junction flyer in my face. "We are not only in the land of the bargain clothing

47

outlets, we are also in the heart of major antiquing," she informed us.

I checked my watch. "Bess, we've already gotten a late start today. We might have to put off shopping until tomorrow."

"Not to worry," Bess said, opening up her tourist map. "The shop I'm thinking of is just east of town, on the same road where the TV crew is headquartered."

George laughed. "She's got all the bases covered, Nancy. You might as well give in."

"Believe me, I'm not about to argue with that famous Marvin logic," I said.

George left us to go for her morning run, then she'd head to back to the café and Winnie's computer. After upgrading the firewall she planned on kicking the café's website up a notch. We'd decided to hook up at Winnie's in the early afternoon.

Bess and I went toward the shop. True to her word, Bess's chosen shopping target, the Antique Attic, was close by. A sign with the word REALTOR was arched over the top of the handcrafted Antique Attic sign.

"Looks like the perfect place for a quick browse," Bess said as we parked next to the shop's pale green minivan.

"*Quick* is the operative word here," I reminded Bess. The storefront had two doors. One door led into the realty office, the other into the antique store.

A buzzer sounded as we walked in, and a tall woman with salt-and-pepper hair looked up from arranging jewelry in a display on the counter. She was an attractive fortysomething: a spare, nicely dressed woman with great cheekbones. I was sure I had seen her somewhere before . . .

But where?

I shook off the thought. I had never been anywhere near here before. How would I know her?

"Just browsing?" she asked. "Take your time. But if there's something in particular you're looking for, feel free to ask."

"Thanks, we will," I said. Immediately a display of beaded bracelets caught Bess's eye. "Would Hannah like one of these?" she asked. Hannah was our housekeeper in River Heights, and she'd been like a second mother to Bess and George ever since she'd become a part of our household.

I examined the bracelets, then shook my head. Bess, however, selected one and left it at the counter with the shopkeeper.

I joined Bess as she examined some items on a table near the counter: baseball caps, sweatshirts, little plastic flying saucers and rocket ships. Also prominently displayed was a selection of really spooky alien masks.

"UFO souvenirs?" I smiled.

The woman behind the counter laughed. "No store

in town can afford to be without them. I, at least, tried to have a few of the more unusual and tasteful items, but they can't help but be what they are."

"Have the UFO sightings brought you business?" I asked, while Bess sorted through the T-shirts. The Antique Attic seemed to have turned into a souvenir shop too.

The woman just shrugged. "Not much. Especially since the roadblock is only about four miles from here. But my rentals have picked up some," she added as the phone rang. As she picked up the phone, she gestured toward a corkboard over a shelf full of old books. I sauntered over and looked at the interior and exterior photos and descriptions of some of the rental properties. Most were for ski chalets, but one in particular caught my eye. Sunk into the side of a hill, the dwelling resembled a well-furnished cave.

The storekeeper came up. "Interesting property," she said. "It's called Under Hill. I just negotiated a short-term lease for it. It'll be free in a month or so, I imagine." Before I could say I wasn't interested, she introduced herself as Eleanor Dorian. "Better known as Ellie," she added.

"Nancy, look over here!" Bess said. "I found the perfect present for Ned."

Ellie smiled at me, then went back to arranging the jewelry. I joined Bess, who was fiddling with the

50

latches on an old black typewriter case.

"Nice!" What a find! My boyfriend Ned had started collecting old-fashioned portable typewriters. Bess had gotten involved in his project using her mechanical know-how to get them back in at least *moderate* working order. "Is the typewriter inside?" I asked, hoping it wasn't. Now considered antiques and not just tag-sale junk, the portables had become a bit pricey for my budget.

"No," Bess answered, finally getting the stiff latches to open. Indeed, it was empty. "And it's for an old 1920s Underwood."

"Like the one Ned found at the university flea market!" I decided I had to have the case. Fortunately, because it was in bad shape, it was cheap.

We brought the case and Bess's alien souvenirs up to the counter. Ellie had already put Bess's bracelet in a little plastic bag, but even before we paid for it, Bess took it out of the bag and slipped it on. "I'll take it like this," she said.

"Was it the UFO sightings that brought you girls here?" Ellie asked as she wrapped Bess's items.

"No way," I answered as I pulled out my wallet. "We came to visit a friend."

"Maybe you know her," Bess said. "She's my Aunt Louise's friend from cooking school. Her name's Winifred, and she—"

Before Bess could finish the sentence, Ellie froze and looked shocked. "You're friends of Winifred's?"

"Sure," Bess said, sounding confused. "We just met her, but—"

"Whatever," Ellie said. She practically threw Bess's package at her. Shoving my change into my hand, she stalked out from behind the display case.

"I think it's time you left now. Any friend of Winifred Armond's is *not* welcome in my shop or home."

She jerked the door open and, with an overblown dramatic gesture, motioned for us to leave.

After a moment's hesitation Bess grabbed her purchases and scurried out the door.

Ellie tapped her foot, waiting for me to follow. Her message might as well have been written on a flashing neon sign: GET LOST—OR ELSE.

Or else what, though? I had no idea. I only knew I felt insulted. I had half a mind to storm out without the typewriter case. I was also tempted to throw it at her.

Instead, thinking of how much Ned would love the case, I picked it up, and with all the dignity I could muster, stormed out after Bess.

Bess climbed into the passenger side of my car and slammed the door hard. I was right behind her, slipping into the driver's seat. "What was *that* about?" she asked.

"I have no idea!" I said as I reached around and placed the typewriter case onto the backseat. Then I remembered exactly where I'd seen Eleanor Dorian's face before. My anger instantly melted away. "Or maybe I do, Bess. . . ."

I turned to face her. "Remember the photo in the café—the one over Winnie's framed good-luck dollar bill?"

"What of it?" Bess said. "I didn't really look at it."

"I did." I had to smile. "Winnie's old business partner." I nodded back toward the shop as I turned the key in the ignition. "That's her. Ellie is Winnie's cousin."

As I pulled out onto the road, I watched out of the corner of my eye as Bess's lips formed a silent "Oh."

"So we wandered into what is essentially the camp of the enemy," I said.

"Huh," Bess said. "It kind of takes the sting out of it—in a way. It wasn't personal. Eleanor just doesn't want to have anything to do with Winnie, or with anyone connected with Winnie."

"What in the world happened between those two women to make Eleanor so bitter, though?" I asked.

"Maybe it's a family feud," Bess suggested.

It was at that moment I checked my rearview mirror. "Bess, we're being followed."

7

Dognapped

Bess craned her neck so she could see who was following us. "It's a white van. And it belongs to . . ."

"*Reel TV!*" I chimed in.

I laughed along with Bess, but inwardly I wondered— was Izzy's crew *already* following us, without our knowing it? The possibility vaguely annoyed me. Izzy had given me the impression we'd check in with the production company at their base before the filming started.

On the other hand maybe the *Reel TV* van wasn't tailing us at all. They just happened to be behind us on the same road, headed for the same destination at the very same time.

I'm not so hot on coincidences—so to be safe, I decided to try to lose them. Just ahead the road forked: The main road leading to Brody's Mountain was to the left. I went right.

"Where are we going?" Bess asked as the road curved sharply around a bend.

"I have no idea," I answered, checking my rearview mirror. As the road straightened out, I felt a wave of relief; I seemed to have lost the van, and it was simple. "I guess they weren't really following us."

"You were trying to *lose* them?" Bess gasped in disbelief. "But why?" she asked. "We all agreed to let them shoot us."

"We did," I conceded. "I just thought we were supposed to meet up with them first at the roadblock— sort of set out the ground rules."

"What ground rules?"

"I don't know. But I want to be sure they have a few—like, would you really have wanted them inside the Antique Attic to document Ellie's little temper tantrum? Or hanging around while we eat?"

Bess considered this a moment. "No, I wouldn't. But, Nancy, speaking of eating . . ."

"You can't possibly be hungry again so soon," I marveled.

"No, but look up ahead. There's a farm stand selling pure maple syrup! Let's stop and get some."

"Bess!" I wanted to protest about us wasting time, but I quickly realized that I was the one who had chosen this detour. "Okay, but . . ."

Bess groaned. "I promise, I'll make it quick."

Then I remembered how much Dad loved Hannah's pancakes drenched in syrup. "Me too." I laughed. "Maple syrup is the perfect present for Dad and for Hannah." I pulled into the driveway and was greeted by the barking of what sounded like a dozen dogs.

I waited a moment before opening the car door, but when no dogs came running, I figured they were penned up somewhere.

Bess and I climbed out and looked around. "This place is great!" she said. "It's like out of a time warp!"

The farm was picture-perfect with its two barns, a silo, and a corncrib filled to the brim from the harvest. It hugged the side of a mountain. Steep, newly harvested meadows flanked a wooded area, dark with pines, while the farmhouse and outbuildings sat close to the road.

Clouds were building over the top of the mountain, and a cold wind whistled through the trees. I wrapped my blue scarf more tightly around my neck and said, "I think that's part of Brody's Mountain."

"Which explains those ski chalets," Bess said. She pointed past the barn, where the driveway continued and branched off, one branch leading up a slope to the meadows, the other leading to a circle of tourist cabins bordering the forest.

I grabbed my purse from the car and followed Bess to the stand. Pumpkins, squash, gourds, and other late-fall produce were attractively stacked in weathered baskets. Several shelves held different-size containers of maple syrup. The stand itself was unmanned.

I hesitated, and wondered if I should scout out the barnyard to see if anyone was around. At first glance the place seemed deserted, except for the sounds of chickens pecking in their coop and a cow lowing in the barn. From where I stood I couldn't see if a car was parked behind the house.

Peeking through the rustic fence that surrounded the property, I saw a stone path that led across the lawn to the house. Deciding I should go and ring the doorbell, I opened the gate, then noticed the sign: NICHOLS KENNELS AND CHATEAU RENTALS.

A NO VACANCY sign dangled beneath. Apparently the UFO sightings had brought business even to this out-of-the-way farm.

"I just figured out why there are so many dogs," I called back to Bess. "These people are breeders as well as farmers."

"And the name Nichols rings a bell," Bess said, holding up one of the containers of maple syrup and showing me the label with the farm's name. "Where have I heard the name before?"

I'd heard it too. Something about the chateau

rentals jogged my memory. As I was trying to recall exactly where I'd heard the name, an elderly man came charging around the corner of the house. He moved with remarkable speed for someone with a pronounced limp.

When he spotted us, he waved his cane in our direction. "My dog's gone missing," he shouted. "He's been dognapped!" He paused. "By those blasted aliens!"

"Dognapped?" I repeated, not sure I'd heard right.

"By aliens?" Bess's eyes widened. The beginnings of a smile tugged at her lips.

The distress on the man's face was so obvious that I knew we shouldn't laugh. I shot a warning glance at Bess. She cleared her throat and turned her face away.

"Don't just stand there, girl!" he snapped at us. "Do something!"

"Like what?" Bess exclaimed.

"Like use one of those portable phone gizmos. . . . My phone's out, and so is half the electricity in the house. They zapped everything," he said.

"'They?'" I tried to sound serious. "Aliens stole your dog? Are you sure he didn't just run away?"

The man waved off my comment. "I may be old, missy, but I'm no fool. Of course I'm sure. I wouldn't stand here saying Sherlock was dognapped if I thought he'd escaped on his own." He tucked his cane under his arm and pulled his wool cap down over his ears. "So are you going to use your phone or not? Every young'un has one. I'm assuming that thing on your belt is a phone, right?"

I unclipped my cell phone from the waistband of my jeans, but I was reluctant to call the police. The dog had probably just run off, and the man was probably caught up in the general local hysteria about the UFOs. "Um, who should I say needs help?"

The man rolled his eyes. He gestured to the sign. "Nichols. Aldwin Nichols, that's who. Just Aldwin will do. And no need to bother with directions. Everyone knows the Nichols farm. And they all know Sherlock, too. He's the best tracker in the county. The sheriff and the mountain rescue crew use him all the time," Aldwin added, sounding rather proud.

Suddenly he looked past my shoulder. "Not them again!" he blurted.

As I turned to follow the direction of his gaze, the *Reel TV* van pulled up in front of the vegetable stand. As the wheels crunched across the gravel, the sound of baying hounds started up from the kennel.

"You were right," Bess murmured.

Without warning Aldwin barged past me. "I told you people to stay off my land." He went right up to the van's front door and planted himself in front of it, barring the driver from getting out.

A guy wearing a baseball cap rolled down the window. He poked his head out, and I recognized him as one of Izzy's crew members who was staying at the inn, but I didn't know his name. Of course, he knew mine. "Nancy, tell him we're here because we're filming you."

Aldwin turned on me. "*You* brought them?"

I shook my head. "I didn't *bring* them. They're following us. I'm not sure why exactly, yet."

The guy reached beside him on the seat, then held a sheet of paper out the window of the van. "Because you signed releases, that's why."

"But Mr. Nichols didn't," Bess said sweetly.

Aldwin just glowered at the van. "Get out of here now. You're trespassing, and I'm calling the police." He reached out for my cell phone, grabbed it, and dialed 911. Once he got someone on the other end of the line, he barked the details of the emergency, then hung up.

The driver of the van ducked his head back in, rolled up the window, and shifted the van into reverse. His partner in the passenger seat was punching numbers into his cell. I watched as they turned around and sped down the road.

"What do you girls want?" Aldwin growled, handing me back my phone.

"Maple syrup?" Bess answered in a small voice.

I jumped in quickly. "And maybe while we're here we can help you find your dog."

He gave me a long hard look, then grunted. "What's your relationship to that bunch?" He gestured toward the van. It was already some distance down the road, rounding the bend and moving out of sight.

"The producer wants to document our reaction to the UFO sightings. Because," I quickly added, "I think they're hoaxes."

"You do, do you?" He snorted. He passed through the gate to the front yard and waited for us to follow him. Then he looked at Bess. "And you, blondie—what do you think?"

I cringed. Bess hated being called "blondie." I could feel her tense up—but she surprised me by smiling at Aldwin.

"I'm not sure," she admitted. "What do you think?"

He gave a tight-lipped smile. "Until today I thought it was all hogwash. But now, after what happened here last night when those lights starting circling up yonder, over the hill—well, I've become a believer." He limped up the stairs onto the porch. "You can see for yourself, though."

He led us out to the barnyard. The kennel occupied a large area, out of sight of the road. I noticed it was divided into three parts, two of which had several large individual dog runs. At the sight of us, young bloodhounds raced up to the fencing, their baying shifting into expectant whines and barks.

"Down, you critters." Aldwin poked his fingers through the links. The dogs scrambled to lick his fingers. "It's not feeding time."

A smaller third pen held a doghouse. I noticed the gate had been left open. The doghouse and pen were unoccupied.

Aldwin walked up to the empty pen. "Like I told you, he's gone missing."

"But what makes you think he was abducted?"

"By aliens," Bess added, examining the cage. "You said he's a really good tracker. Is it possible that a hunter stole him?"

Aldwin snickered. "Do you really think a tough watchdog like Sherlock is going to just head off with some stranger?"

I wasn't about to argue—but any dog can be lured by a raw juicy steak. And wasn't an alien a stranger? "Okay, so he wouldn't let a stranger take him, but obviously someone—or something—did, Aldwin. What makes you think it had to do with our supposed space visitors?"

Aldwin leaned against a stump and launched into his story. "Sherlock's been acting kind of off for about four weeks now. . . . That's when the first UFOs came to town. He'd been baying at nothing and heading back that way into the woods," he said, pointing to the area where we'd sighted the supposed UFOs the other night, "anytime he was left off his lead."

"That's unusual?" Bess asked. She was petting one of the dogs through the fence.

"For him? Absolutely. He's trained to stay in the barnyard when he's loose."

"When he went into the woods, did he seem to be tracking something or someone?" I asked.

Aldwin nodded. "Mind you, whatever he was tracking, he never ventured *far* into the woods. I figured someone was probably camping where they shouldn't. Illegal campers usually set up just far enough into these woods not to be visible from the house or the road. The forest is deep, and it's too easy to get lost.

"Sherlock is pretty protective of the farm and generally stays within its bounds. Occasionally he crosses into the state forest that surrounds and borders us, but not by more than twenty yards or so."

I made a mental note to scope out the forest while it was still light today, or tomorrow. Anyone camping would leave some kind of evidence. Sherlock sniffing out campers certainly made more sense to me than his being dognapped by UFOs.

"But, like I said, Sherlock seldom goes out of the

barnyard. But lately he'd started going over there pretty regularly. I didn't think a whole lot of it, until last night. I was in the middle of my chores when those lights turned up again over the mountain." Aldwin stopped and pointed at me. "Like you, I thought they were some kind of trick. But Sherlock started howling—set the whole pack baying. I managed to get him inside his pen and tied him up good. All at once there was a big blast of light. Never seen that happen before. Scared me a bit. I raced into the house to call the police. In the middle of dialing, though, the electricity went out, the phone died, and Sherlock stopped howling."

"We didn't lose electricity in town," I told him.

"You didn't?" He seemed surprised. "Maybe I did because the farm's closer to those UFOs."

Bess nodded. "That makes sense. They probably emitted some sort of electrical interference."

Aldwin gaped at Bess. I had to smile. Not only was Bess going along with Aldwin's story like any good detective would, but she was also showing off her gift for all things mechanical. She adores delving into the mysteries of how things work and is a real Ms. Fix-it.

Aldwin finally went on. "This morning when I checked the dogs, Sherlock was gone. At first I thought I'd left the pen open, but the latch was still closed, and there were no dig marks beneath the fence. And here, look for yourself—no animal around these parts leaves tracks like this."

He showed me into Sherlock's pen. Tracks crisscrossed the soft ground. Some I recognized as paw prints from a rather large dog, which I assumed were Sherlock's.

Aldwin saw me staring at some footprints leading from the opening of the pen to the doghouse. He pointed to his own boots. "Those there are mine. But I didn't want to step over those tracks there. . . . I was hoping the troopers would come and check them out."

I hunkered down to examine the ground. Besides the paw prints and boot prints, there were others— the strangest tracks I'd ever seen.

8

Proof Positive?

I **noticed the ground** was dotted with geometric marks: circles, hexagons, squares, diamond shapes. On closer inspection I noticed there was another kind of print—not paw print, nor geometric mark, nor boot print. These prints were from webbed feet, each one about four inches long.

The sort of print a duck might make.

I was about to ask if Aldwin had ducks, wondering why he hadn't noticed, when something about them caught my eye. Sure they were webbed, but unlike bird prints these had evenly spaced ridges. They looked like something from a factory; they were definitely not the work of Mother Nature.

"What do you think, Nancy?" Bess asked. I hadn't noticed her enter the pen behind me. She crouched lower and touched my shoulder. "What made these?"

"I have no idea," I answered.

"Me neither," Aldwin said. "But maybe these folks do."

I looked up in time to see a trooper car pull up to the farm stand.

Captain Greene climbed out. I was relieved to see him. Maybe he'd have a practical explanation for Sherlock's disappearance and for the mysterious prints.

He shoved his hat onto his head and ambled across the yard. "Aldwin, what's up?"

"Sherlock," Aldwin exclaimed. "He's gone missing."

"You called me to look for your dog?" Captain Greene frowned. "That's not like you."

"Maybe not, but it's not like Sherlock to get dognapped either."

"Dognapped?"

"By aliens," Aldwin stated.

"Dognapped? By aliens?" Captain Greene folded his arms over his burly chest and studied Aldwin's face. I suspected he was waiting for Aldwin to laugh. "Aldwin Nichols, are you trying to pull a fast one?" the captain finally said.

"Rupert, I know this sounds crazy, but old as I am, I've still got all the tools in this shed," he said, patting his forehead. "You know that."

"What I *know* is that you love practical jokes." He

paused. I imagined he was waiting for Aldwin to admit the dognapping was a prank. Aldwin just kept his lips pursed.

The captain lifted his eyebrows. "You claim Sherlock is the victim of an alien abduction?" the captain asked, still incredulous.

"I swear it's true. Ask the girls here. I showed them evidence."

The captain caught my eye. I just shrugged.

Then Aldwin launched into his story. I watched the captain's expression shift from amused to confused to downright skeptical. "No one else lost electricity, Aldwin; there's got to be an explanation." The captain turned to the other trooper. "Caleb, go check out the phone lines and electric wires going into the house."

"I checked already," Aldwin said. "Nothing's been cut, if broken lines are what you'd be looking for. I'm happy to show you exactly what I didn't find!"

While he and Caleb circled to the back of the house, Captain Greene turned to me. "Nancy, what brought you here?"

"Shopping, actually," Bess said, and she introduced herself. I had forgotten that she hadn't met the captain the night before.

Captain Greene tipped his hat in an old-fashioned gesture, then turned back to me. "Of course the whole story doesn't hold water."

"You don't believe him either," I said.

"It's a pretty outrageous claim. Still . . ." The captain rocked back on his heels, then lifted his shoulders. "I'm beginning to wonder. This is the first claim of an abduction. If it weren't Aldwin making the accusation, I'd say it's just hysteria. But he's a pretty down-to-earth fellow. I've known him since I was knee-high to a termite. He may be a prankster, but he's no liar. Besides, he generally likes to stay out of the spotlight."

Bess chuckled. "We noticed. He sure chased off that TV crew."

"Good for him," the captain said. "Forget you heard me say that, though. Lots of people in town are thrilled with the idea of Brody's Junction being the location for a reality TV show."

"I'm sure the TV crew will be back when they hear about a dognapping," I said.

"Yep," the captain agreed. "Once the grapevine starts buzzing with news of Sherlock's abduction, they'll be back for sure. This time, though, they'll keep off Aldwin's property. They'll set up on the road or on state land and use those high-powered cameras. And I won't be able to stop them. The mayor's given them pretty broad rights with their permits."

We walked with the captain over to the dog pen. He gentled the baying hounds with his voice. "Down boys. It's just me." They seemed to know him and paid no attention as he examined Sherlock's pen. I didn't know if I felt relieved or disappointed when he declared the prints were nothing like anything he'd come across.

He walked out of the pen, but didn't latch it. "I'll have Caleb cordon off the area, then get some of those Feds to check this out. Maybe they should dust the latch for prints, then photograph the tracks—maybe even make plaster casts."

As we headed back to the cars, Caleb and Aldwin were still in conversation on the porch. "Are you still thinking of checking out the meadow where the sighting took place?" the captain asked me.

"I'd like to. Izzy said if we were going to be filmed, I'd have more access to the area."

"Not to the meadow. It's sealed off like a crime scene," he said. "You still need official permission."

"From you, I bet," Bess said.

"Yes, and I'm more than happy to have you look at it, Nancy. I spoke to Winifred about you, and she told me you really are a serious detective back in River Heights. It'll be good to have an unprejudiced eye look over things."

"I don't know if I'm unprejudiced," I admitted. "I'm going to need some pretty serious convincing that this whole deal is for real."

The captain checked his watch. "You'd better get over there before noon. The weather looks like it's going to close in quickly. Before long, snow could blanket the area."

"What about Izzy's crew?" Bess reminded me.

"Trust me, they'll find us soon enough," I said, not really in the mood to make Izzy's life easier.

Bess picked up three small jugs of syrup at the stand, leaving the money in the coffee tin. Meanwhile, the captain radioed ahead to alert his men. After the call, he told me, "The FBI folks are all so tight-lipped about all this spaceship business, it makes me wonder if there really is something to it."

He gave us an alternate route to the meadow, to elude the *Reel TV* crew, then we left. The trip was short; soon we emerged at a paved county road, blocked off by trooper cars.

After checking my ID the officer in charge let us pass. "Oh, you can go through," he said. "You're the girls the captain just radioed me about."

Half a mile down the road we reached our destination. The perimeter of the meadow was cordoned off with yellow crime-scene tape. We parked on the shoulder and got out. Only one of the police cars nearby was occupied. When we pulled up, a trooper got out to check our IDs, but he seemed to have been expecting us.

As I tucked my driver's license back into my wallet, he told us we could explore the meadow's borders and get a pretty good look at burn marks on the grass. But he warned us not to go under the police tape and not to touch anything.

"The FBI is still collecting evidence," he said. I looked and saw a black unmarked car parked farther up the road. No agents were in sight.

"This place gives me the creeps. I'm glad I'm not on night shift," he said.

I wondered if the UFO sightings happened only at night, but before I could ask, his radio crackled to life, and he ducked back into the car to answer it.

"So what exactly are we looking for?" Bess asked as we clambered up the embankment. It was tough work. The meadow had been harvested recently, and sharp stubs of cornstalks jabbed through my jeans. Between the harvested rows, the furrows were deep, and even with hiking boots it was hard to walk. Poor Bess was wearing only thin-soled sneakers.

"I'm not sure," I answered. "I want to see those burn marks close up. But I also wonder if anything dropped off those supposed UFOs that might give us a clue as to who made them."

Bess laughed. "You refuse to believe they really are from outer space."

"Why would UFOs—supposing there are such

things—bother coming to an obviously less technologically advanced place like Earth? Tell me that. Also, why would the aliens kidnap a dog?"

"Because they don't know enough about us—maybe they think dogs are the dominant species on our planet."

I was about to protest, when I caught the expression on Bess's face. Her eyes were laughing, and she was barely suppressing a grin. "Bess Marvin, I'm serious."

"I'm not," she admitted cheerfully. "But that doesn't mean I don't believe these sightings might be for real."

"Then you can help try to prove it. Let's split up. You head over that way." I pointed to where the meadow dipped down the side of the hill. "I'll check out the edge near the woods."

With a cheery wave Bess began making her way around the margin of the field just outside the police tape. The meadow dipped, putting Bess out of my sight line. I set off, not sure what I was looking for.

After walking a few yards, I spotted a distinctly charred area of flattened grass and cornstalks. It extended about two feet from just inside the cordon.

I tried to picture what could have caused the mark. A spaceship blasting off was what my mind was telling me, but another voice inside still said "nonsense."

I knelt and tried to touch the singed stalks, but I

couldn't reach far enough under the police tape. My fingers, however, brushed the nearby grass. When I drew back my hand, my fingertips were coated with a smelly, powdery dust. The pungent unpleasant odor reminded me of something I'd smelled before. But what?

I knew I'd remember eventually. I wiped my fingers on a tissue and stuffed it into my pocket, then continued around the rim of the field. Soon I reached the stand of tall pines and slender birches that marked the start of the forest, possibly the same forest that bordered Aldwin's land. The smell of burned foliage was even stronger there.

I noticed the highest branches of the trees were angled sharply away from the meadow—again, as if a wind had pushed them aside.

How had someone managed to wreak all this havoc on the field and forest?

I was flummoxed. If this was a part of a hoax, it had been brilliantly executed.

And if it wasn't a hoax, then what was it?

A chill went up my spine as I was forced to admit the truth: Maybe the UFOs were for real.

9

Trashed

No sooner did the thought cross my mind than I felt the hairs at the back of my neck rise up. I sensed I was in danger.

"UFOs only turn up at night!" I uttered the words aloud simply to calm myself.

Just then I heard the snap of a branch breaking behind me.

I whirled around and gasped. "Mayor Brody!"

His face half-shadowed by the pines, the tall man smiled sheepishly. "Sorry, didn't mean to startle you. The trooper down by the road told me you were up here, scouting out the scene of the crime, so to speak." He sounded genial enough, but he had scared the daylights out of me.

"You didn't have to sneak up on me like that."

"You do seem a bit jumpy" was his response. "Which makes sense, considering what happened on the Nichols farm. So we've finally got you convinced that our space visitors are the genuine article."

"What makes you think that?" While my reservations about the existence of the UFOs were fading, I was far from convinced.

He had the courtesy to look embarrassed as he admitted, "I overheard you just now. Talking to yourself—about UFOs not appearing during the day."

"Yeah, well, I just thought I was alone" was all I said.

"Being alone up here gives me the jitters too." He stepped out of the shadows and into the sun. "It's pretty amazing, all the damage they've caused."

"I was thinking the same thing," I confessed. "Have there been any strong lightning storms recently that might have burned the grass?"

The mayor frowned. "Seeing all this, you're still skeptical?"

"Yeah, I guess," I answered. "For instance there's this weird smell in the air."

The mayor sniffed. "Very unpleasant."

"Very *chemical*, and very familiar," I pointed out. "Would creatures from outer space have the same chemicals we do?"

"Why not? The whole universe is made of the same elements," he said. "Though I am a retired high school chemistry teacher, I assume that's general knowledge."

Did he think I was ignorant of basic science? I felt my temper rising, but I managed to keep my tone even as I said, "Yes, it is, but would some advanced civilization necessarily combine chemicals in the same way we do?"

"Good question," he said. "But, truth is, there are only so many—" A loud shout echoed across the field, cutting him off.

"Hey, you! Get out of there, *now*!"

We both spun around. Three troopers, guns drawn, were racing up the embankment. They weren't rushing toward us, though—they were running in the opposite direction.

"Bess!" I gasped, and darted back up the rise.

I arrived just as Bess was crawling out from under the police tape. "I just wanted to get a closer look," she said. She spotted the guns and paled.

"Put those guns down!" the mayor ordered.

The troopers instantly obeyed. The one who'd checked us out earlier approached Bess. "I told you to stay outside of the cordoned area."

Bess visibly gulped. "I know, I know." She hazarded a smile. "I got carried away. I wanted to get closer to feel the alien vibes."

Her dimples worked their usual magic. The trooper's stern expression softened. "Don't do it again."

Bess dropped her eyes and looked repentant, but I noticed her surreptitiously slip something into her pocket.

Turning to me, the mayor seconded the trooper. "You were given free run of the crime scene, with some clear rules, Nancy. Mess up again, and we'll bar you from the site. I don't care who wants you investigating what," he added.

Did he and Captain Greene share some negative history? I made a mental note to find out from the innkeeper later.

I made the appropriate apologetic remarks, then steered Bess to the car. As soon as we were inside, I asked, "What was that about 'alien vibes,' and what, exactly, did you put in your pocket?"

Bess began to grin. "Sounded good, didn't it? Actually, I wanted to get a closer look at this." She pulled a piece of glittery metal out of her pocket.

"What is it?" I asked, instantly curious.

She handed it to me. "I don't know. When the sun came out, I spotted it in the grass. I just had to check it out."

While I was driving, I couldn't really study the metal shard. I gave it back to Bess, then told her, "Bess, you've just taken evidence from a crime scene."

78

"There's been no crime, Nancy. The UFOs haven't hurt anyone."

"Have you forgotten Aldwin's dog?"

Bess shook her head. "Of course not, but that just happened today. I bet the troopers haven't even found out about it yet."

"They probably know," I said, without thinking. "The mayor did."

"How did he find out about it so fast?" Bess asked.

"Chatter over the police radio, probably. No doubt he has a receiver in his car." I refused to let Bess divert my attention. "The mayor and Sherlock aren't the point here. You shouldn't have taken this piece of junk from the meadow. It may be important."

"If I bring it back," Bess said, before I got a chance to say she should, "they'll ban you from your investigation for sure. Besides, there was more of it."

"Where?"

"All over the place. It just doesn't show up unless the sun hits it," she said.

That's why I'd missed it. The sun had been ducking in and out of the clouds all morning long. Maybe I'd find some closer to the woods but outside the restricted area. As soon as I could, I'd go back to check.

As I headed back to town, the white *Reel TV* van came barreling down the other side of the road, heading back toward the meadow. I watched it disappear around the curve.

Bess chuckled. "They managed to miss filming a pretty good scene up there."

"I'm glad," I said. "Imagine having troopers threatening you, immortalized on video tape." Then I remembered something. "I thought they didn't have access back here."

"Someone changed the rules, I guess," Bess said, then moaned. "Would you look at this?"

I glanced away from the road. She was holding up her foot. Her new sneakers were covered in some kind of dark goo.

"You must have stepped in something nasty back there in the meadow," I told her as she rummaged in her bag for a tissue.

She wiped her shoe, then groaned. "I don't believe this!"

"What's the matter?" I asked.

"It's some sort of paint." She scrubbed at her shoe some more. "And it stains, big-time," she mumbled. "Maybe Winnie has a stain remover back at the restaurant."

Bess was still lamenting the state of her new sneakers when we pulled up in front of Winnie's café.

A small crowd was gathered outside the entrance, and a black-and-white town police patrol car was parked in front. Winnie stood in the doorway, looking distressed. As I parked, George spotted us and hurried over.

"You won't believe what happened!" she said as I jumped out. "Someone broke into the restaurant in the middle of the night. They trashed the place."

Bess and I followed George into the restaurant. Tables were overturned, and baked good were scattered around the floor. Jars of jams and jellies were knocked off the shelf; shards of glass were everywhere. It was a complete mess!

The only things that weren't broken or overturned seemed to be the display cases, and this surprised me. These vandals were oddly selective.

Winnie had brought the policeman inside. Joel Scarletti stood beside her, looking equally distraught.

"Officer Cargill," she was saying, "who'd do this?"

"It's all my fault," Joel told the officer. "I finished the baking at about three a.m. The front was all locked up, but when I left out the back, I didn't lock the door. I rarely do, because no one's ever broken in before."

Officer Cargill pursed his lips. "Don't be so hard on yourself. No one locks doors around here—but now with the flood of tourists and such, we're just going to have to change our ways."

The officer went off to talk to some workers in the kitchen. I decided to check the back door. It dangled half off its hinges, and the frame had been partially ripped apart.

"What's wrong with this picture?" I asked Bess as she and George walked up.

"More like what's wrong with the door," she said. "Winnie's going to need a new one, that's for sure. In the meantime I could do some temporary repairs on this one."

"I'm sure Winnie will appreciate all the help she can get, but my question is, why in the world would a thief wreck the door trying to break in, when it wasn't locked to begin with?"

"Whoever did it probably just wanted to cause Winnie more trouble," George said. She sounded angry. "Whoever did this was just plain mean. No money was taken. Fortunately, I had locked the computer under the counter, or that would have been vandalized too."

"It wasn't vandals," Officer Cargill declared from inside the restaurant. He was standing in the short passage that led from the kitchen to the back door and the alley. "In fact, it wasn't even a *who*." He paused, and I could see him struggling not to laugh. "It was a *what*."

"You mean the aliens?" Bess gasped.

Officer Cargill caught my eye and began to chuckle.

I cracked up as the pieces of this particular puzzle

snapped into place. Winnie hurried up to us and looked at me in dismay. "Sorry, Winnie," I gasped when I was able to get my breath. "The place is a disaster area. But this time round, it wasn't sabotage. Your culprit lacked hands, but sure had claws."

"Good for you!" The policeman looked at me with respect. "I'm pretty sure I know what happened. Your assistant here was baking. The pies probably smelled good. Bears sometime wander into town. This one wandered right into your kitchen."

Winnie sagged against the wall, relief evident on her face. "For some reason that makes this mess easier to deal with—though the bear couldn't have had worse timing. How will I ever get this place together before dinner? I'm booked solid."

"We'll all help!" George offered.

"And so will lots of other people," a young woman spoke up from the doorway. I saw that she wore an apron emblazoned with the logo of the pizza shop next door. "I'll round up a few guys to do the heavy work. That'll free up your people to man the kitchen." Several other shopkeepers chimed in, offering help.

"I'm good in the kitchen too," George reminded her. "I'm not my mother's daughter for nothing."

"No, George," Winnie said softly as we walked back to the front of the café. "I'd rather have you concentrate on the computer. This might have been the work of a bear, but my computer woes were caused by humans!"

I was about to offer my services, when with a screech of brakes a battered pickup truck came to an abrupt stop in front of the café. A stout, elderly woman climbed out of the passenger side with a bit of difficulty, but once she was on the sidewalk, she moved with surprising speed.

She marched right up to Officer Cargill. "First the dog," she exclaimed, her blue eyes furious. "Now Aldwin. He's gone missing! Can't imagine what aliens— or anyone else, for that matter—would want with the likes of Aldwin, but there it is: He's gone!"

10

Close Encounter

Addie May Nichols, you're making no sense. Slow down. Tell me exactly what happened." Officer Cargill tried to take the woman's arm, but she shook him off.

"If I knew *exactly* what happened, I wouldn't be here, would I?" she replied testily.

"Probably not," he said. I could see he was trying to humor her. "But start from the beginning. What's all this about your brother going missing? More to the point, what in the world does this have to do with one of your dogs?"

Upon hearing the officer's words, I instantly realized two things. This woman was Aldwin's sister. And while the mayor knew about the dognapping, the officer didn't.

I found that latter bit decidedly odd. Almost as odd

as seeing who chose that moment to slide out of the driver's side of the pickup truck.

I recognized him immediately as Nathan Blackman. That's when I remembered where I'd heard of the Nichols farm. Blackman was renting one of the farm's chateau cabins.

He leaned back against the cab of the truck. His expression was decidedly amused as he watched Addie May begin her story.

She explained how Aldwin discovered Sherlock had been dognapped. "Then, after the troopers left, Aldwin came into the house. I was in the basement doing laundry. When I came back upstairs, he was gone. At first I thought he'd headed off to look for Sherlock, but then I found his cane on the porch. He couldn't have gone far without it."

"Probably those aliens teleported him clear off the porch," Nathan said, his voice mocking.

Though I still wasn't sold on the alien abduction scenario, I couldn't stand Nathan's sarcastic tone. "And exactly what do you think happened to Aldwin?" I challenged.

He shrugged. "Beats me. First a dog goes missing, then the dog's owner. Maybe it really is aliens, or . . . who knows? So many new folks in town could mean some foul play."

I found Nathan's suggestion curious. I couldn't shake

the feeling that the guy was up to no good. Then again, maybe I was being unfair. Just because he looked scruffy and eccentric didn't mean he was up to no good.

I had learned a long time ago to trust my instincts, though—and my gut feeling about Nathan Black-man said there was more to him than met the eye.

The more I thought about it, the more likely it seemed that a science fiction writer might very well benefit from living in a town where aliens were rumored to abduct people and their pets. It was the perfect place to write an eyewitness report. With the publicity he'd boost his chances of getting a more lucrative deal for his next book.

Since he lived on the Nichols farm, it would be a cinch for him to lure Sherlock away. As for Aldwin . . . I shuddered at the thought. Luring either of them might be easy, but keeping them hidden would be nearly impossible—unless he had done them some real harm.

I decided I had to get back to the farm and some-how check out his cabin when he wasn't around.

Just then Addie May stood up straighter. Apparently, talking to Officer Cargill had calmed her some. They shook hands, and I overheard the officer tell her that perhaps Aldwin got a ride from someone who offered to help him look for the dog. With any luck he'd be home by the time she got back to the farm.

"I doubt it," Addie May said, "but just in case, I'd

better head home now. I sure hope you're right, Larry Cargill."

As she and Nathan left, I realized I'd have to wait to search the writer's digs. I could check him out on the Internet once George's computer was available, though. With that in mind I went back inside. George had righted one of the tables and was doing something to Winnie's laptop. As I approached, she looked up.

"Just the person I want to see," she said. "Can you give me a lift back to the inn?"

"Aren't you going to work on Winnie's website?"

"I am," George said. "But I've already transmitted all the files I need from her computer to mine. I'd rather work in the quiet of our room than here," she explained.

"I'll get Bess," I said.

When I found her, Bess was in the middle of fixing Winnie's back door. Joel was holding the door in place while Bess secured the bottom hinge to the newly mended door frame.

Bess glanced up at me, taking in the car keys in my hand. "I need to finish up here," she said. "I'll catch up with you later."

I dropped George off at the inn, and after grabbing a warmer jacket and a flashlight, I decided to go back to the meadow. This time I was determined to evade not only the *Reel TV* crew but the police. I asked George if she could google up a map of Brody's Junction.

"Sure," she said. A minute later she had surfed her way right onto the site of the county's highway department and downloaded a map depicting every back road within twenty miles of Brody's Junction.

George printed out the map on her portable printer. "Good luck," she said, handing it to me.

Stuffing it into my pocket, I doubled down the stairs and ran smack into Izzy Sanchez. "Where were you this morning?" she asked. "I mean *after* that dognapping incident, which, by the way, will make great footage. My guys are on the scene now."

"So they already know about Aldwin going missing?" I asked, avoiding her original question.

Her eyes widened. "That old farmer?" She sounded shocked, but I had a hunch she knew all about Aldwin's abduction. "Did they get him, too?"

"Whoever 'they' are, yes, they did. If your guys want to help find him, they should check their footage for clues—that is, if he went missing after they began spying on his farm." The fact that I'd emphasized the word *spying* didn't escape Izzy's notice.

"Nancy, why are you so negative about the show, about us, and more important, about the aliens?"

I felt like I was being interviewed, but then I reminded myself I had signed the release. "Off the record?"

She gave a reluctant nod.

"Okay. I like reality TV shows just fine. But I never wanted to be on one. In some ways I'm a private person. I only agreed to let you film me so I could prove the sightings are faked."

"And what have you found so far?" Izzy asked.

"I'm not sure," I answered. I wasn't ready to admit to her I was beginning to consider that the sightings might be the real McCoy.

Izzy shrugged. "Off the record, where did you hear about Aldwin going missing?"

"In town, from his sister." Suddenly inspiration struck. I'd figured out how to divert Izzy. "But I'm surprised your crew wasn't there to cover the break-in."

"We're already spread pretty thin. They can't be every-where," Izzy said, then frowned. "Wait a minute—what break-in?" This time her surprise seemed genuine.

"At Winnie's café. You should check it out. Some people are blaming it on the UFOs." I purposely didn't mention a thing about the bear.

"Uh, thanks," Izzy said, sounding puzzled. She pulled out her cell and speed-dialed someone. When I walked away, she was talking quickly to whoever was on the other end. I climbed into my car convinced that I'd sent her on a wild goose chase and maybe wrangled some time alone away from *Reel TV*'s prying eyes.

Using George's map, I chose my route and headed off. Frequent checks in my rearview mirror proved my theory was right. I had ditched the TV crew, at least temporarily. All too soon, though, they'd learn that Winnie's break-in had nothing to do with aliens—real or imagined.

My route took me past Aldwin's farm and the vegetable stand. As I went by the vegetable stand, I slowed down and took a good look out the window. The pickup truck was parked in the circular drive in front of the rental cabins. Nathan and Addie were already back home.

According to the map, the road in front of the Nichols place encircled Brody's Peak. A small logging road cut through the state forest that bordered both Aldwin's land and the area I'd explored earlier, behind the roadblock.

Looking for the logging road, I drove past the farm, the cabins, and a WELCOME. BRODY'S PEAK STATE FOREST sign. The country road continued up the hill. After negotiating a hairpin turn, I spotted the logging road. I turned onto it but parked a few yards in from the main highway. The dirt road was too deeply rutted for my low-slung car to manage, so I had to make my way back to the meadow on foot.

Since I wasn't interested in exploring the forest itself, I decided to leave the logging trail. As I trekked uphill toward the meadow, I made sure I kept the paved road in sight. The last thing I needed was to get myself lost and become the subject of a mountain rescue.

As I neared the meadow, the trees thinned but were replaced by stands of dense brush. To my right I spotted the gleam of sun on metal. Trooper cars, I realized. At the same moment I heard the voices of the state police officers manning the roadblock.

As they chatted companionably, I managed to approach unnoticed. I moved as quietly as possible, watching where I stepped, careful not to tread on any fallen branches.

With the troopers distracted I decided I could risk a more careful inspection of the meadow. Bess said that pieces of metal like the one she'd found were all over the place. If I found more of them, maybe I'd be able to figure out what they were.

Hugging the shadows of the pines, I crept forward. From the shelter of the brush and trees I saw the glint of something shiny in the grass. To reach it I'd have to crawl beneath the police tape—and hope the troopers were still distracted by their own conversation.

I took a deep breath and was about to kneel down, when to my left something rustled in the brush.

I froze. Had the troopers followed me?

The rustling grew louder, and a pungent odor wafted in my direction. Heart pounding, I turned around . . .

And found myself face-to-face with a huge black bear.

11

Unusual Suspects

I **gaped at the** bear. The bear gaped back.

We both froze.

He stood so still, he resembled one of his stuffed relatives at the River Heights Natural History Museum. His nose twitched, though: a clear reminder he was no more stuffed than I was from Mars. And he smelled awful, like a person who hadn't bathed for a year.

As the bear sized me up, I almost hoped a UFO would materialize and abduct me!

Vanishing into thin air apparently also appealed to the bear, because at that moment it bolted away, crashing like a runaway semi through the brush. I bolted in the opposite direction, making an even bigger racket.

I tore back toward the logging trail, with no thought of evading the troopers. I heard them laughing above the sound of my panicky footsteps. Obviously they'd heard the ruckus in the woods. "Guess a bear spooked someone. Probably one of those campers," one voice said.

"Should we go check it out?" a second trooper asked.

"Nope. The bear did it for us," the first voice answered. "Doubt they'll be snooping around up here again."

They were so busy laughing, they didn't even bother to look my way as I ran toward the logging trail.

I was halfway up the trail before I let myself slow down. I was pretty sure I had set some new world record for a through-the-forest dash, and I was still breathing hard when I got back to my car.

A welcoming committee was waiting for me, consisting of Mayor Brody, a state trooper, and, oddly enough, Izzy. Apparently my attempt to lead her on a wild goose chase back to Winnie's hadn't worked. Her cameraman, Frankie Lee, was with her. He held a video camera on his shoulder and was already filming.

"Nancy, are you okay?" Izzy asked. She sounded concerned, but she motioned to Frankie to keep the camera rolling.

"I'm okay," I said, brushing my hair off my face. "I just had a run-in with a bear."

"Ah, a bear," she said. "This is bear country. But you know that already."

Mayor Brody cleared his throat. "You're lucky that's all you ran into." He looked more annoyed than worried.

"As opposed to aliens?" I shot back. I was coming down from a serious adrenaline rush, and my patience was wearing thin.

"Both Nichols and his dog have been abducted," the mayor snapped. "Clearly, something dangerous and out of the ordinary is going on in this town."

All too aware this sequence was being filmed, I tried to tone down my response. "Yes, I'm aware of that. Which, by the way, is why I was in the woods." I turned to the trooper. "Have you searched this area for something other than signs of space invaders? Has it occurred to anyone that Aldwin and his dog might be the victims of foul play of the human kind?"

The trooper looked insulted. "We know how to do our job, Ms. Drew. We're always on the lookout for illegal campers, but we haven't found any recently, or even signs that they've been up here. All we've turned up lately are more of those tracks, like the ones we found at Mr. Nichols's farm."

"You found tracks like the ones in the kennel? Here, in the woods?" This was news to me.

"Not in the woods," Mayor Brody said, "but in the meadow. Not that we owe you an explanation."

The state policeman looked grim. "You, miss, had

95

no right to bypass that roadblock and traipse around on your own up here."

"I had permission," I said, resenting being scolded.

"You weren't given free range," the mayor said.

"Sorry, Ms. Drew," the trooper interjected. "The situation has grown more dangerous over the past twenty-four hours. With folks vanishing into thin air, we're tightening our security. No one's allowed up in this area, and that includes you."

"But Captain Greene said—"

"He's been overruled," the mayor told me.

I wondered by whom. Part of me wanted to press the point, but I was still too shaken up from my encounter with the bear to argue. Besides, I didn't like the idea of Izzy filming *Nancy versus the Mayor*. "Okay" was all I answered.

"I'm going back to the inn," I told the film crew as I got into the car. "You can follow me there or not, your choice. You can hang around outside my room, or find something better to do while I hit the shower." I slammed the car door and drove off.

I arrived back at the inn still peeved and with the stench of bear in my nostrils. But a hot shower followed by a generous dousing of Bess's aromatherapy body lotion did a great deal to cheer me.

I came out of the bathroom and found George putting a file folder and CDs into her knapsack. Her laptop was open on the dresser. "You look better," she remarked, looking up as I reached for my lucky blue sweater.

"I feel like a new woman!" I told her as I finished dressing, then stashed Bess's souvenirs and the maple syrup on top of the wardrobe.

George grinned. "You should have worn that earlier. Maybe it would have kept away the bear."

"Or the aliens," I laughed. I showed George the typewriter case I'd bought for Ned at the Antique Attic.

She eyed it approvingly. "He'll love it," she said. "Too bad it's too heavy for my laptop."

"You'd probably start a trend," I said, looking for a place to stow it. Finally I settled for the top of the wardrobe next to Bess's souvenirs.

"What's happening with Winnie's website?" I asked.

"All done!" George answered. "I finished tweaking it. Now when people google restaurants in Vermont, hers will be right there in the top two or three." George slipped into her moccasins and got up and stretched. "Better yet, I installed enough high-powered software to safeguard her computer from all but genius hackers. When we get back to the café, I'll adjust the security settings for her broadband connection. One reason she got hacked is that she hadn't secured her wireless network."

"What in the world does that mean?" I asked.

"I'll show you," George said. She turned on her laptop. After it booted up, a little window opened, informing us that other wireless networks were in the vicinity. George clicked her mouse again. "This is a list of networks within range of the gizmo that lets me connect wirelessly to the Internet—it's called a router," she explained. I noticed each network had a name, ranging from arbitrary numbers and characters, to nicknames to real names. Some of the names were followed by the icon of a padlock; others weren't.

"Some are labeled 'unsecured,'" I noticed.

George nodded. "Right. Newbie users don't realize that leaving their networks open means that anyone in the neighborhood can use their service, and with even minimal know-how someone can hack into their machine—even into their e-mail."

"That can't be legal," I objected.

George shrugged. "It depends. There are some people who leave their networks open on purpose, just to encourage free traffic on the Net. But hacking definitely breaks the law. I wouldn't hack into someone's system unless it was absolutely necessary. However, I did write a program that lets me 'sniff' around other people's computers—I've used it to help you solve cases before."

"I don't want to know the details," I protested,

getting a distinctly uncomfortable feeling that any kind of hacking by anyone other than the government was breaking the law.

"You wouldn't understand them anyway. But just by hitting this key sequence I can get there."

"It's my phone number!"

George grinned. "Clever, isn't it?" She punched in her password.

"Hey, could I get on there for a minute?" I asked.

"Sure," George said, handing me the computer. I went online to check out Nathan Blackman. The search engine quickly led me to his fairly sophisticated website.

"Who would have guessed?" George remarked as she looked over my shoulder at the screen. "He's a real science fiction writer."

"Published by some pretty decent houses, too," I noted. He had a few good reviews, but there wasn't much personal information on him. I scanned the list of his titles. "All his books are about UFOs, George. And aliens." I scrolled down further. "Here's one called *The Roswell Hoax*."

George looked thoughtful. "To write that," she said, "he'd have to investigate the how-to of hoaxes." She tapped the screen with her finger. "But look: This guy prefers to write on an old 1940s Underwood typewriter rather than a computer. It sure doesn't sound like he has the ability to fake the sightings, Nancy."

"He could always be in cahoots with someone else who had the technical know-how to fake sightings."

"But who?" George asked.

"Someone else who would benefit from the publicity," I answered.

George chuckled as she shut down her computer. "That's only about half the business owners in this town." She frowned. "But seriously, *if* Blackman faked the sightings, how exactly did he do it? And who would have had the know-how to help?"

"I've been thinking about that." I took my notebook out of my purse. I turned to the page where I'd copied down the info about UFOs that I'd googled the night before. "Apparently all you need is a helium balloon, a fishing rod, and a small flashlight. You turn the light on, put it inside the balloon, and inflate it with helium. Tie it with a long fishing line—"

"Sure, the plastic filament kind—that wouldn't be visible," George added.

"Right. I guess that's attached to a fishing rod, so you can move it around. You hold it out the window of a car and move quite fast on a back road, and *voila*—glowing, floating spheres."

"Wow, that's pretty low-tech," George commented.

"Low-tech enough for Nathan to pull it off on his own."

I went back to my notebook. "If you want it to crash, you can shoot it down with a BB gun. The whole idea can work on a bigger scale too, with a weather balloon—though you'd need more than one person to move an object that size."

"What would be *really* cool is if you used one of those flashlights that you use in emergency work—the kind where the light pulses."

I cracked up. "You're not supposed to be inspired by all this."

George winked. "Hey, it all could be fun."

I checked over my notes. "Besides hoaxes, of course, there are genuine mistakes. For instance the government might be testing some new top secret aircraft. If people saw the craft when light hit it in a certain way, they would think it was a flying saucer."

"And of course, officials would deny its existence," George said. "Maybe that's why the FBI is here. Maybe there's no hoax, Nancy. Maybe it's some kind of government cover-up."

"Could be."

"But you don't think it's likely," George stated.

"Not likely, no." I shrugged. "If they aren't genuine spaceships, then I'm sure they're part of some kind of scheme to benefit someone."

"And you think that someone may be Nathan Blackman?"

I nodded. "But all I have is a hunch and no evidence."

"Then our next step is to get some," George declared.

We decided our first stop would be Winnie's café, to see how she was doing. If the place was back in decent shape, and if Winnie could spare her, we'd pick up Bess.

Afterward we could go together to check out Nathan's cabin. I knew it wasn't a good idea to confront Nathan Blackman on my own in such a deserted place. If he happened to be home, so much the better; a conversation with the science fiction writer might give me a better idea of exactly what he was up to—if anything.

We left the inn, and within minutes we were back on Main Street. The entrance to the café parking lot was blocked by an idling minivan with no driver inside. I began grumbling about inconsiderate polluters who didn't give a hoot about the environment, but I broke off when George spotted a parking space.

George and I got out of the car and were headed down the sidewalk when a woman's shrill scream pierced the air.

"Up there!" she shrieked. "Up there!"

I looked up and shielded my eyes. Bands of gray

clouds half-masked the afternoon sun, but the gray-ish sky was still bright.

After a second I spotted a slender disk hovering above Winnie's café. First it hung suspended in silence over the café, and then it zoomed upward with a loud whooshing sound. The spacecraft suddenly shifted to one side, then U-turned back east and vanished in a flash of light.

"That's the second daytime sighting. The first one I got on tape!" Izzy's voice sounded out behind me. It was only then I realized that the whole time I was observing the UFO, a camera was panning around me and the crowd.

"What's your reaction?" Izzy asked.

I braced myself to give some sort of noncommittal answer. As I turned, I saw her holding a microphone up to another onlooker. Maybe she'd given up on me.

I didn't bother to listen to the man's response. Instead I caught George's eye and telegraphed that we should ditch Izzy while we had a chance.

We braved the crowd that had gathered, and grad-ually made our way to the café. Winnie was standing outside, and so were Joel and Mary Beth, the waiter. Where was Bess, though?

"Did you see that?" Winnie was clearly shaken. "It hovered right over the roof. I was scared to death that it would crash right into the building!"

"Winnie, it's okay. The café's okay. All that happened was the lights flickered," Joel said, trying to calm her. But he looked upset too.

"Maybe we should just forget about dinner tonight and—"

"No," Joel told her. "We've already done all the prep. You can't waste the time or money, Winnie. We've got to tough this out tonight. Meanwhile, all the UFO did was rev up exposure for your restaurant. Let's take advantage of it."

Winnie slowly nodded, then opened the door and led us inside.

I took one look around and gasped.

The place looked great. A new batch of baked goods was displayed behind the freshly polished glass of the case. The tables were neatly set for the next meal. A few spots on the wall behind the counter were the only evidence that the place had been trashed the night before.

"Where's Bess?" I asked as George unearthed the software CDs she'd brought for Winnie's computer.

"Is she in the back?" George asked, coming out from behind the counter.

Winnie frowned. "I haven't seen her since before the UFO sighting." She headed Joel off as he passed by. "Have you seen Bess?" she asked him.

"Sure. She was right here a while ago." He

scratched his head. "Wasn't she outside just now with the rest of us?"

"I didn't notice," Winnie admitted. "Maybe she's still working on the back door."

Joel shook his head. "She finished." Then a light-bulb seemed to light up above him. "I know where she is. She went outside to put the trash in the Dumpster. She was probably in the alley when the UFO showed up."

"I'll go get her," I volunteered. "You should get back to your cooking," I told Joel. "Sounds like it's going to be busy tonight!"

I walked down the short hallway leading to the back entrance. I pushed open the door and saw the Dumpster but no Bess. I called her name, but no one answered. Maybe when the UFO had turned up, she'd run up the alley to join the crowd on the sidewalk?

From where I stood I could see people still discussing the sighting. I had started toward them when I spotted a single red sneaker, stained with brown paint.

Even before I picked it up, I knew—it belonged to Bess.

12

Alien Abduction?

As I bent to pick up the sneaker, I caught sight of something glittering under the Dumpster. My heart leapt into my throat as I knelt down and pulled out a beaded glass bracelet. I recognized it at once as Bess's latest purchase. No sooner had I retrieved it than Joel came out of the kitchen.

He immediately saw me kneeling on the ground. His eyes went from the bracelet in my right hand to the sneaker in my left. "Where's Bess?" he asked, his face going pale.

Without stopping to answer, I jumped up and ran to the mouth of the alley. A trooper's car was parked outside the restaurant, and half a dozen people were still gathered outside the café. Bess wasn't one of them.

I hurried back into the alley. Joel was pacing aimlessly in front of the Dumpster. "I knew something like this might happen," he cried, his voice pure panic.

"What do you mean?" I stepped right in front of him.

He stopped pacing. "They found her," he said.

They? It was all I could do not to shake him. "Who?" I shouted. "Who are 'they'?"

"The aliens." He stated it so matter-of-factly that for a moment I almost thought he'd witnessed her abduction.

Then I came to my senses. "Joel, just because we all thought what we saw was some kind of flying saucer doesn't mean that Bess was carried off by creatures from outer space."

"You don't understand. They *knew* where to find her," he declared.

Had the guy totally lost it?

"You don't believe me, do you?" He didn't give me a chance to answer. "She showed me that piece of their ship."

I was about to ask what piece when I remembered the shard she'd filched from the meadow. "You mean that bit of metal?" Had Bess really shown it to him?

"Yes," he said. "It was probably embedded with some sort of electronic signature that led them to her."

Joel's conclusion left me momentarily speechless.

"Where in the world did you get that idea?" I

107

finally asked. It sure didn't sound like something Bess would think up.

"Ms. Sanchez, from *Reel TV*. She turned up not long after you left, to check out the vandalism at the café. She had the idea UFOs were responsible. She was pretty annoyed to find out it was just the work of a bear with a sweet tooth. Anyway, she was standing right next to us when Bess showed me her souvenir. At first Bess didn't realize she was being filmed—but then Ms. Sanchez interviewed her and took pictures of the metal."

As I listened, I promised myself that when I found Bess, I would strangle her. What had she been thinking?

Turning to Joel, I told him, "I understand where you're coming from, but you might be jumping to conclusions."

"Am I?" he asked, distraught. "One minute Bess is taking out the trash; the next minute a UFO appears over this very spot. Next thing you know, she's missing. What's your explanation?"

"I have none," I said flatly. "But an alien abduction is pretty far-fetched." Before he could disagree, I told him, "Whatever happened to Bess, we'd better notify the police *now*. After that I'm going to go look for her myself."

I quickly found George inside. "We've got a big problem," I told her. "Bess has gone missing."

George laughed. "You mean she's gone off shopping and forgot to tell us?"

"No." I showed George Bess's shoe and her bracelet.

George exhaled sharply. "What happened to her?"

With George I knew I could be blunt. "Since Bess wouldn't run off leaving one shoe and her favorite bracelet lying in an alley, it's a pretty good bet she was taken somewhere against her will."

George closed her eyes for a moment and took a deep breath. "Okay, I'm not going to panic over this," she announced with a tight smile. "But tell me you don't think UFOs are involved—*please.*"

"I'm not even sure they *are* UFOs. I've got a hunch that somebody wants people to think the population of Brody's Junction has been targeted for the latest rash of alien abductions."

"So then even extraterrestrials—if they actually exist—are innocent until proven guilty," George quipped. "One problem, Nancy—do we have other suspects?"

"Not exactly," I admitted. "But I have a few hunches. He's not exactly a suspect, but I think it's time we checked out Nathan Blackman. He lives in an isolated place, and he certainly had more than one opportunity to abduct both Sherlock and Aldwin. Maybe he also has Bess. Before we look into it, though, we've got to report Bess's disappearance to the police."

"Right," George agreed. She knew as well as I that

time was of the essence. Even if this were some sort of prank, the people involved might panic—and Bess and Aldwin could be in serious danger.

Both the police chief and a state trooper were already seated at a café table with Winnie. As they talked, the officers took notes. Winnie looked beyond distraught. Figuring she'd somehow heard about Bess, I walked right up and interrupted. "Do you know where to start looking?" I asked the chief.

He glanced up from his notebook. "Excuse me?"

"There's a good chance she's wearing only one shoe. It matches this one." I held up the sneaker.

Winnie's eyes widened. "That belongs to Bess. She couldn't get the paint off of it. . . . Wait. Why would the police be looking for her?"

"You haven't heard," George said. She quickly filled Winnie in.

Winnie's face registered pure horror. "This is going too far!" she said, her voice shaking. Meanwhile, the trooper put a call out on his walkie-talkie, then left to secure the alley.

The chief stayed behind.

"Do you think this is connected?" Winnie asked him.

"With what?" I inquired.

Winnie looked desolate. "The recipe book I had on the counter is missing."

"Since when?" I asked.

Winnie shook her head. "Who knows? I know it was here last night when I left. But in the commotion this morning I didn't notice if it had been knocked off the counter. And I didn't realize it was gone until now, when I had to check some ingredients."

"You're sure no one threw it out in the cleanup?" the chief asked.

"Why would anyone throw out a perfectly good loose-leaf binder? Besides, everyone who works for me knows the book is priceless."

George winced. "I remember you said last night that you hadn't finished putting the recipes into the computer."

"Truthfully, I'd barely started. Knowing you were coming, I was going to ask for your help scanning them in." She heaved a sigh. "They're irreplaceable, George. They're my family's old recipes, and I had the only copy. Worse yet, all the café's trademark dishes are from that book. Without the book—well, I don't know what I'm going to do."

As I listened to Winnie, I had a hunch as to her book's whereabouts. "Not to worry," I told her.

The police chief looked up sharply. "You sound like you know what happened."

"I don't, exactly, but one thing's for sure—a bear didn't steal it." Before anyone could even make the suggestion, I added quickly, "Neither did the aliens."

13

Unidentified Friendly Object

Just in case Bess turned up back at the café on her own, I gave the trooper my cell phone number. Then I left with George to try to track her down myself.

Before heading for the car, I checked out the entrance to the café's parking area. As I'd suspected, the minivan had been replaced by a police sawhorse.

"Are you still fixed on investigating Nathan Blackman first?" George asked.

"He's our best bet, but we're going to visit someone else first. I've got a hunch that we might be able to find Winnie's recipe book en route," I answered as we drove out of town.

"I feel bad for Winnie, but can't that wait? Bess is more important than any dumb book."

"No question," I agreed. I knew she was itching

to do something, *anything*, to find her cousin. I felt the same way. "But checking this out will just take a minute," I told her. "Plus, I can't shake the feeling that the missing recipe book is somehow connected to the UFO sightings—and to Bess's disappearance."

"What's the connection?" George asked.

"Winnie's cousin."

"No way!" George exclaimed. Then she exhaled sharply. "Wait, Ellie was Winnie's original partner in the café."

"And after the way she booted Bess and me out of her shop this morning, I'm sure there's some serious bad blood between them."

"Okay—that gives her motive to sabotage Winnie. But why would Ellie kidnap Bess?" George asked. "Or anyone else—and how?"

"That's what I can't figure out. But we're about to ask her," I said as we approached the Antique Attic.

"It's going to feel pretty awkward if you're totally wrong," George pointed out.

"Tell me about it." But as I pulled into the drive-way, I saw the proof that I wasn't wrong. I pointed to the shop's green minivan parked in front of the garage. "That van looks just like the one that was blocking the lot behind the café earlier."

"I didn't really notice," George admitted. "But there's gotta be more than one green van in this town."

"Right. The van I saw might not be Ellie's. Even if it is, it doesn't prove she stole the recipe book," I conceded. I grabbed Bess's shoe and bracelet and started toward the antique shop. On impulse I did an about-face and detoured toward the van. I felt the hood of the car; it was warm.

Maybe my hunch wasn't so off.

"Here goes nothing," George murmured as I opened the shop door.

Inside, Ellie was tallying receipts. At the sight of me her welcoming smile faded fast. "What are you doing back here?"

"I need to talk to you," I answered.

"*I* don't need to talk to *you*. In fact, perhaps you didn't get the message earlier: You aren't welcome here. So leave."

When I didn't budge, she reached for the phone. "This is private property. If you don't leave now, I'm calling the police."

I shrugged. "Be my guest," I said. "Though I'm not sure you want to do that."

George exhaled impatiently. "What Nancy is getting at is, we want the recipe book back—the one you filched from Winnie's café."

"What recipe book?" Ellie asked, looking baffled. But I noticed her hand move away from the phone.

"Your family recipe book—the one you and Win-

114

nie used in the café. The one you stole this afternoon." I watched her face as I spelled it out.

"I was here all afternoon," she declared, looking indignant.

"Oh, then someone borrowed your van?" I suggested.

Ellie's forehead furrowed into a frown. "No one borrowed my van, and what's that got to do with Winnie's book? If that woman can't keep track of her things, that's her problem. It's sure not mine anymore," she concluded bitterly.

"That's weird. I'd think you'd be just as upset as Winnie that someone had made off with your family's recipe book. It's the only copy, after all." George looked right at me. "Isn't that the impression you got, Nancy?"

I nodded, watching Ellie struggle to come up with a response to George's remark. I knew we'd caught her in a lie, but that wasn't enough. Bess was missing, and we needed to get to the root of what was going on. "Ellie, stop denying it. No one's going to press charges against you if you return the recipe book now. We'll just bring it back to Winnie."

Ellie's expression darkened. "Okay, you're right. I did take it. This afternoon. And yes, I was in town with my van. What's all this to you, anyway?" she fumed. "I've got as much right to it as Winnie. It

115

originally belonged to our grandmother. When we decided to dissolve the partnership in the restaurant, the recipe book conveniently went missing."

"Oh, gimme a break!" George scoffed.

Ellie stormed out from behind the counter. "Oh, sweet Winifred Armond didn't tell you that part, did she? It takes *two* people to make a business work—and to make it fall apart. Everyone thinks I'm the bad guy here, but Winnie's no angel. The book must have turned up again, because her menu is totally based on the recipes. She continues to profit from everything we dreamed of and started together. The café was as much my passion as hers. When we split up, she was supposed to copy the recipes and share them. Has she? No!"

I had no patience for Ellie's rant. "That's all history, something you should have worked out before now. Instead you've stolen her book. I bet you also hacked into her computer, tampered with ingredients in her kitchen . . . and who knows what else you've done to get back at her?"

"How about breaking into the place last night and making it look like the work of a bear?" George suggested.

"That's nuts. I didn't break in. Bears have broken into several restaurants around here . . . private homes, too. Leave it to Winnie to try to blame that on me."

"The point is that you admit you stole the recipes. What about the other attempts to undermine her business?"

Ellie's bravado suddenly collapsed. "Okay," she said. She heaved a tired sigh, and threw the papers she was holding down on the counter. "I'm sick of this whole feud anyway. Yes, I stole the book. And yes, I want Winnie's business to fail, so I managed to play a few dirty tricks. As for her computer . . . that wasn't my idea."

"Whose, then?" George asked.

"My son started tampering with her system before he went back to school. He's in Boston, studying to be a programmer. He seems to be able to access her machine from there. It's a mystery to me how."

Her confession encouraged me. It was time to play hardball with this woman. "If your son's such a techie, then he probably helped you on the other front."

"What other front?" Ellie asked, sounding genuinely startled.

"The UFOs," George answered. "We're pretty sure they're a hoax, and since the sighting this afternoon gave you cover to steal the book—"

"Whoa!" Ellie snapped to attention. "You think the UFOs are a hoax?"

I nodded.

"And you think *I* have something to do with

it?" She suddenly didn't look the least bit tired. She looked furious. "Are you accusing me of somehow faking all these sightings?"

"With help, of course," I said, holding her glance.

Dumbfounded, Ellie gaped at me. It took her a second to find her voice. "That's totally off the wall. Forget the *how* of it. *Why* would I do something like that?"

"To rev up business," George suggested, pointing to Ellie's display of alien souvenirs.

"Oh, that's brilliant!" Ellie laughed tightly. "In order to sell more dumb alien masks, I'd try to perpetrate some impossible hoax involving little green men."

"Not for the masks," I told her. "For your realty business. UFO sightings promise to turn Brody's Junction into Vermont's version of Roswell, New Mexico."

"Interesting concept," she said, looking impressed. "But believe me, the last thing I want is to turn this town into a permanent tourist mecca—attracting all the crazies who think they see spaceships ready to invade—"

George broke in. "You're telling us that you had nothing to do with the sighting this afternoon, and Bess's kidnapping?"

Ellie looked confused. "Someone besides Aldwin and his prize hound have gone missing?" I watched her expression morph from shocked to horrified. "Wait, isn't Bess that blond girl who was in here earlier today?"

"Yes," I said. I was finding it hard to read Ellie's reaction. Either she truly was in the dark about Bess or she deserved an Oscar for Best Actress.

"I can't believe it—who'd do that?"

"We think it's whoever is behind the hoaxes—and I'm not convinced you aren't involved with them somehow," I told her.

"Are you insane?" she practically shrieked. "I have nothing to do with the hoaxes, and I have no idea what happened to your friend—but if someone abducted her, that's beyond awful. It's . . ." She was suddenly at a loss for words.

Ellie looked and sounded so dismayed that I found myself sure she was telling the truth: She was certainly in the wrong for sabotaging her former business partner, but the woman seemed totally incapable of perpetrating a UFO hoax, let alone kidnapping Bess—

"Wait," she said, interrupting my chain of thought. "Not being local, you wouldn't know this, but Aldwin is famous around here for being a prankster. When he and the dog went missing, I figured he was taking a joke too far. But if your friend has really been abducted, then Aldwin has too."

"You have me convinced," I finally told Ellie. "You don't know anything about how Bess or anyone else disappeared."

"But you *did* steal those recipes, and unless you want us to turn you in to the police, you'd better return them to Winnie," George said firmly.

"No way!" Ellie declared. "I'm not returning them to Winnie, not until I have copies."

"Then we'll have to call the cops and tell them about how you've harassed Winnie and her café, trying to drive her out of business." George pulled her cell out of her pocket.

"You can't do that," Ellie declared hotly.

"Yes, we can," I contradicted her. I waited a beat before adding, "Unless you go over there now, own up to what you've done, and return the recipes."

George spoke up. "If you do, I'll sweeten the deal for you. I'll input the recipes into her computer and make a disk for you—if Winnie doesn't object. But only if you include a good, heartfelt apology with your very sincere confession."

"All right," Ellie said reluctantly. "I'll go later."

"More like *now*," George said. She turned to me. "Ellie can drive me in her van. You go ahead and keep looking for Bess. I'll meet up with you later at the inn."

Ellie closed up her shop as I left the store. I pushed

the speed limit and headed right out to the Nichols farm.

When I arrived, I parked in front of the farm stand. The front yard gate creaked as I opened it, and the sound sent the whole kennel barking.

"Oh, keep quiet," I cried, feeling annoyed, frustrated, and, deep down, scared about what might have happened to Bess.

The dogs continued to bark as I knocked on the front door, hoping Addie May was still home waiting for Aldwin's return. But no one answered. I figured I'd better check the backyard.

I hurried down the porch steps and rounded the corner of the house, only to find myself eye to eye with the barrel of a shotgun.

And the shabby man pointing the gun at my chest was none other than Nathan Blackman.

14

The Missing Link

Face-to-face with a shotgun, I swiftly weighed my options—not that there were many. Addie's truck was not in the barnyard, so it was a good bet I was alone.

Bolting was out of the question. So was a good karate kick; the gun might go off, and one of us would surely get hurt, if not killed. I had only one choice: I'd have to talk my way out of it.

Before I could open my mouth, though, Nathan lowered the gun. His scowl, however, remained as dark as the lowering sky.

"What are you doing here?" he challenged. With his free hand he turned up the collar of his red wool jacket.

"I might ask the same of you," I snapped.

"I live here." He paused. "What's your excuse?"

"I'm looking for Addie May," I said, trying not to feel foolish. Blackman was right of course. He *did* technically live on the farm. That didn't give him an excuse to accost me with a gun, though.

He leaned the gun against the side of the house and folded his arms across his chest. "Well, she's not here." He jerked his head toward the barnyard. "See for yourself. Her truck's gone."

"Right."

"She went into town to check in with the police. Fat good that lot'll do. She actually thinks they'll find her brother."

Nathan had given me the opening I was looking for. "What do you think?" I asked.

He shrugged. "I'll tell you what I *don't* think. No way aliens whooshed down here to the old farmstead and 'napped an old lame farmer and his dog." He narrowed his eyes and studied my face. "You think somewhat like I do. There are no UFOs—no real ones, at any rate—secreted back there in them there hills!" He grinned as he mocked a television backwoods accent. Then, as quickly as his grin had appeared, it vanished. "So why are you snooping around here?"

"Because I think the UFOs are a hoax, and I have a feeling you know something about the whole scam."

He surprised me by nodding slowly. "I do."

Was he so ready to admit it? Suddenly I was terribly

conscious of that gun. If Nathan confessed to perpetrating such a major con, why would he stop at kidnapping just two people? Might as well make it three!

"Aren't you going to ask me exactly what I know?"
he asked.

"Please. Tell me," I said, trying to sound skeptical
instead of frightened.

"If you don't mind, I'd rather do that someplace
more comfortable." He looked up toward the sky.
"A storm's brewing, the temperature's dropping, and
standing around, I'm getting cold."

Without waiting for my answer, he picked up the gun.
Holding it barrel down to the ground, Nathan started
back toward the circle of cabins behind the barn.

When I didn't follow, he turned around. "Aren't
you coming?" He hesitated, glanced from to me to
the gun, then grinned. "Not to worry. I'm not about
to hang you out as bait for the so-called aliens. And
I won't hurt you. The gun's for hunting. I was on my
way to see if I could bag a deer when I heard the
dogs barking. I came back up here to see who was
lurking around the house ... given what's been going
on here lately. Anyway, I'm not the bad guy here."

I wasn't convinced. At the same time, standing in
the cold wind was quickly getting old. I wondered
if I actually had a choice. Would he let me just walk
away and leave?

As if reading my mind, he said, "Hey, whatever you decide. Stay. Go. I'm going back to the cabin with or without you." With that, Nathan turned and stalked past the kennels. The dogs stopped howling and began to whine with delight, their tails wagging furiously as they jumped against the chain-link fence to greet him.

"Wait up," I called, making my choice. No way was I going to let the chance go to corner this guy. Besides, if Nathan Blackman put his gun down and out of reach, we'd be on more equal footing if he decided to play rough. I knew a few martial arts moves.

Inside the cabin he propped the gun against the wall near the window. He shrugged off his jacket and walked over to the tiny kitchen area. "Want something hot?" he asked, plugging in the electric teapot.

"Sure," I said.

While he fussed with mugs, I looked around. The cabin was small but pleasantly decorated, with framed prints on the wall and country curtains on the windows. Pretending to be interested in the delicately printed fabric, I walked over to the window and glanced down at Nathan's rifle. I wasn't all that familiar with guns, but could see that the safety was on.

At least he wasn't careless with firearms. I began to think his story about going hunting might have been true.

The rest of the cabin was simply furnished: A daybed

was shoved against one wall, one easy chair sat in the middle of the room, and a couple of end tables that had seen better days sat on either end of the daybed.

Everything felt tidy and clean—except for the antique writing desk tucked in the corner. An ancient typewriter was barely visible through the chaos of papers, pencils, and coffee mugs that cluttered the surface. Stacks of books were piled haphazardly beside and under the desk and on top of the folding metal chair.

The typewriter didn't resemble any in Ned's collection of old-fashioned portables: It was large, the type I'd seen in old movies set back in the mid-twentieth century. Blackman definitely seemed averse to technology.

I glanced over as Nathan poured hot water into two mugs, dropped a tea bag in each, and handed me one. "So, you never really answered me. What do you think happened to Aldwin and his dog?" he asked, and sat down on the edge of the daybed. I settled into the one chair.

"The same thing that just happened to my best friend Bess," I said, carefully watching his face. "Someone kidnapped them."

For a moment he seemed to turn to stone, then he slowly put his mug down on the table. "Someone else has gone missing? A girl?" He sounded and looked appalled. "This has gone too far," he said very softly, looking down at his hands.

"What? What exactly has gone too far?"

His head snapped up. He stared at me, understanding written on his face. "You think *I* had something to do with all this?" When I didn't respond, he shot me a look of pure disgust. "How could you?"

"You yourself admitted just now that you have some kind of inside knowledge about the UFO hoax," I told him.

He bristled. "I didn't say that. I have an idea of how the con men are pulling it off, but that doesn't mean I'm involved in it—or that I'm sure exactly who is involved. But when it comes to the abductions, I'm as much in the dark as you."

"Convince me."

"How can I convince you about something I don't know?" He glared at me.

"Start with what you do know." I needed to find Bess fast, but I had no idea where to look. Nathan seemed my best lead yet. I had to hear him out. Maybe he'd let something slip that would help me find her.

"Did you see the sighting in town today?" he asked.

I was surprised *he* had, but I simply nodded yes.

"Me too—from here. This time our visitors' ship made noise, as I'm sure you noticed. The daytime ones always do. Here's why." He got up and, in spite of the state of his desk, quickly located a catalog. "I ordered this shortly after the first daytime sighting." He handed me the catalog.

It was for remote control model planes. "What do these have to do with . . ." I broke off as the truth dawned on me. Hobbyists operate remote control planes from the ground. The planes themselves are large—usually transported by their owners on trailer hitches or in the back of pickup trucks. I looked at Nathan Blackman with newfound respect. The man was brilliant. "Someone altered these planes to make them look like UFOs."

"One plane. It would take a lot of work, but it could be done," Nathan pointed out. "The planes are usually built from kits to begin with. A clever, very handy person using lightweight materials could probably make the plane look like your typical science-fictional flying saucer."

I put aside the catalog and looked at Nathan. "And the planes are noisy. There's a model plane airport back home. Neighbors always complain about the racket."

"Of course, at night there is no noise. Whoever's perpetrating the hoax isn't using those remote control planes at night. They're using some other trick, so that there's no noise. A little spookier. Not sure what that could be, but I'm working on it."

"I'm impressed," I told Nathan. "But what made

you even think of ordering this catalog?" If the man was smart enough to think up such a scheme, surely he could find an accomplice to help him work it out. If Bess hadn't also gone missing, I would have bet on Aldwin—now that I'd learned he was the town prankster. He'd make himself appear abducted with Nathan's help. But Aldwin wouldn't have kidnapped Bess, I was sure of that.

"The daytime sightings have been in several locations. That means someone can cart the remote control UFOs around. The nighttime ones are always only over the meadow. Why? I haven't been able to figure it out. Two different methods of faking it—I'm sure of that much."

I had to point out the obvious. "You do realize that telling me this makes you even more suspect?"

"When it comes to figuring out how to fake it, sure. But not of kidnapping anyone. Besides, if I were the bad guy here, why would I let you in on my supposed secret? To top it off, you're looking at a guy who can't even program a VCR or work a DVD player, let alone build a model plane."

He was so blunt I found myself inclined to trust him—but I needed to know more. "I heard you came here to write," I told him.

Nathan then told me he usually booked the Nichols cabins while he was on deadline for a book. Instead of peace and quiet, this time he found himself in the middle of a circus, thanks to the UFO sightings. He almost left, but found himself intrigued at first by the townsfolk's reactions, then by trying to figure out how the sightings were faked.

Intriguing as his story was, it didn't bring me closer to finding Bess, and I told him so.

"Whoever's behind this has upped the ante in a pretty nasty way," he said, scratching at his beard. "But why?" Then he answered his own question. "I bet her good looks up the publicity ante as well."

"Publicity for whom? The town, the *Reel TV* people . . . ?"

"Sure, why not. Like they say, follow the money—and it's big-time bucks for the TV crew, and—"

I stopped him in midsentence. "Wait. Izzy, from the TV crew, saw that Bess had taken a souvenir from the location of the UFO sightings."

Nathan cocked his head. "Up by the meadow? Now *that's* interesting. So your friend found a clue there. Whoever took her wanted to be sure that evidence never came to light."

"I know, I know!" I cried. "But the problem is, where did they take her? I'm not even sure who 'they' are. It could be Izzy's crew. But who knows who else Bess showed her treasure to."

Nathan got up. "I don't know, but I do know this

much. Every one of the nighttime sightings happened over that meadow. Someone has some way of hanging out there. And it isn't obvious to anyone, even now with the FBI on the case."

As Nathan spoke, I began to get a niggling feeling. Something I saw or heard earlier in the day held the missing clue, but what? I looked out the window. Daylight was fading fast. It was late afternoon, and between the cloudy skies and the short early winter day, it was growing dark.

"I'm going back there now," I said, zipping up my jacket.

"It's going to be dark soon!" Nathan warned.

"That's why I'm going now. No one can see me," I told him.

Nathan reached for his jacket and his gun. "Do you want me to go with you?"

"No. I'm better off on my own." I wasn't sure whom I could trust now. Nathan's suspicions had raised my doubts about all the town officials, as well as about the *Reel TV* people. And a small doubt lingered in my mind about him.

He jotted down his phone number on a piece of paper. "If you need help, call."

I said I would, then even gave him my cell phone number before I set off.

It was dark enough to turn on headlights, but not

quite dark enough to explore the meadow unseen. I decided to check in with George as promised, and at the same time pick up warmer gear since a storm was brewing.

Minutes out of the Nichols's driveway, a distant bright light in the sky caught my eye. For a moment I thought it was a plane, but it began to circle lower and lower.

Another UFO hoax?

I kept driving toward town, but then I realized the shiny disklike object wasn't hovering over the meadow. Instead it seemed to be traveling in the same direction I was, just high up over the road.

I began to have the impression it wanted me to follow it. "Nancy Drew, you're losing it!" I told myself, but my curiosity wouldn't let me ignore it. What harm could it do to pursue this latest version of the hoax? In fact, I suddenly realized, maybe whoever was manipulating it would accidentally lead me to themselves, and even to Bess.

Almost as soon as I decided to follow, the saucer picked up speed and veered to fly above a side road, one that traversed the forest just west of the roadblocks. Caught up in chasing it, I turned onto the dirt road, which quickly turned into something closer to a rutted track as it climbed up the steep side of the mountain.

My car's engine was up to the task. Its low-slung

profile wasn't. Just when I thought I'd have to give up and somehow back my way down, the road widened slightly. The flying object seemed to explode in a flash of blue light, then was gone. Just ahead, my headlights illuminated the wide expanse of the meadow. Instantly I doused my headlights. For sure they would have been visible to anyone for miles.

Clouds covered the stars, and it took a moment to get my bearings. It wasn't until I stepped out of the car that I realized the world suddenly seemed silent. Suddenly—because the UFO I'd just encountered hadn't been silent at all. It hadn't whooshed like the one earlier, but through my car window I had heard it emitting a low-pitched constant but loud hum.

Then I thought of the bear. I was about to turn around and drive away when I told myself any bear would have been quickly scared off by the car and by the flash of light in the sky.

Working up my nerve, I headed for the meadow. I took out my penlight and aimed it at the ground. Glowing in the dark just ahead was the yellow police tape. I ignored it and stepped beneath.

The circumference of the charred circle of grass was only a few feet away. I bent down to pick up a small piece of singed cornstalk—but it wasn't singed at all. It was sticky. When I looked at my hand, my fingers were covered with paint. It looked and smelled like the kind of red-orange paint used to rustproof metal.

Conscious that every minute on the meadow increased the chances I'd be discovered, I debated a moment about looking for more of Bess's souvenir shards. Suddenly, out of the corner of my eye, I saw light bobbing on the hill across the way. It looked like someone was walking, holding a flashlight.

I turned off mine and watched the bobbing light get lower and lower to the ground. Then it disappeared. Someone fell down, I figured. I waited a moment for whoever had fallen to get up.

They never did, though. It was as if the side of the hill had swallowed them up.

Puzzled, I returned to my car. Back at the inn I'd look at the map to see what road led to that hill across the way. I hadn't seen house lights, but maybe a farm lay below the rise. I'd have to check by daylight. Whoever did live there had a good view of the UFO sightings.

As I climbed into the car, my cell phone rang. Nathan was my first thought, but when I answered, it was George. "Nancy! I figured it out. . . ."

"Me too," I told her. "Or at least with Nathan's help—*how* they did it. It's all a hoax, for sure. What did you come up with?" I asked, starting back down the road and attaching my hands-free earpiece to the phone.

"Thanks to my trusty laptop and all those unsecured Internet connections I told you about, I know not only the *how* but the *who*. Get back here ASAP—Oh darn, someone's at the door." With that, George hung up.

What had George found? She sounded excited, nervous, but not particularly frightened. It made me think that whatever she'd learned, she knew Bess would be okay. For fear of being stopped by the cops, I forced myself to stay within the speed limit. I still made it to the inn in record time.

I raced upstairs and threw open the door. "George!" She wasn't there. The lights were still on. The phone was on the bed, where George had left it with the receiver on the hook. George's backpack was on the dresser, and her cell phone was still beside it.

A blast of cold air made me look over at the window. Why had George left the window open? Then I remembered the fire escape. I hurried over to look out. Below, the extension ladder at the bottom of the fire escape had been lowered. It led right to the inn's service entrance and back parking lot.

After closing the window, I looked around the room. Nothing was in disarray. Nothing had been stolen. George, however, was definitely missing—and I was pretty sure it wasn't by her own choice.

15

StarWoman

George hadn't just gone missing—she had been taken, probably by whoever had snatched up Aldwin and Bess.

I reached for the phone to call the police, but then remembered Nathan's suspicions, as well as my own. Anyone in town might be involved in these abductions.

It was then I remembered George's laptop.

When she'd phoned, she had mentioned that she had used her laptop to find who was behind the hoax. I looked around, but it seemed to be missing—or had she stowed it in her backpack?

I got up to check, and stubbed my toe on something by the side of the dresser. I looked down. It was the typewriter case I'd bought for Ned. That was weird. I was sure I'd put the case up on top of the wardrobe along with Bess's bag of souvenirs.

Had George moved it? I picked it up. It was heavy. When I unlatched the cover, I found the laptop inside. Before George had answered the door, she must have stowed it away. Why? I had no idea, but I thanked my lucky stars she had.

I booted it up. George had mentioned using someone's unsecured Internet connection. If I could follow her cybertrail, maybe I'd find a clue that would lead to her kidnappers.

I logged on, using George's password—she'd shared it with me a while ago. Instantly a little window opened on the right-hand side of the screen, listing networks in range. Two were secured, one wasn't.

George had shown me that my phone number activated her sniffer program—the one that allowed her to access someone's computer through a wireless system and eavesdrop on their cyberconversations. I took a deep breath and punched in the numbers.

Immediately I found myself looking at an IM exchange. Someone with the screen name Star-Woman was chatting with Lightmaster.

I couldn't believe what I was reading.

StarWoman: Where did u stow her?
Lightmaster: Underhill. Cramped quarters. Not safe.

StarWoman: Hang tough. We r almst there. All will pay off big time.
Lightmaster: If we don't end up doing time.
StarWoman: No way. Today café nice FX.
Lightmaster: Last hurrah! RC broke right after. Last time though. Parts unavailable two weeks.

So Nathan had been right. Whoever Lightmaster was had disguised a remote control hobby plane as a UFO.

Underhill . . . underhill. Why did that ring a bell?

As I watched the screen, the IMs stopped. Had StarWoman figured out she was being sniffed?

On the off chance that was true, I closed up George's machine and put it into my backpack. When I left the room, it was coming with me. If George had other leads stored on her computer, I couldn't risk someone stealing it.

As I put Ned's typewriter case back up on top of the wardrobe, the sight of Bess's souvenir bag triggered my memory. "Under Hill!" I gasped out loud. Of course. It was the name of that rental property posted in Ellie's shop. The pictures had grabbed my attention. It was built into the side of a hill, and Ellie had said someone was renting it for a few weeks.

Earlier, when I had watched that bobbing flashlight disappear into the side of the hill, I had thought someone had fallen. Unlikely as it seemed, that someone had probably entered an underground house. If that person was Lightmaster, then I knew where to find Bess and George.

I had no intention of waiting until morning. I pulled out a map, and in a few minutes I'd located the back road leading to the meadow—the same one I'd been on earlier. From there it was easy to figure out what township road led to the hill across the way.

I grabbed a hat, a warmer sweater, and a larger flashlight. Then, grabbing my pack, I plunged into the hall and, as I was wriggling into my parka, ran right into Izzy.

"Hi. How are things going?" she asked.

"Um, okay. But I'm in a rush." Suddenly I remembered her room was next door to ours. StarWoman was the perfect screen name for an egotistic TV producer. . . .

Was her running into me just an accident?

Izzy gave a dramatic little shiver. "I can't imagine going farther than that blazing fireplace downstairs on a night like this. It's starting to snow," she added.

"I didn't realize," I said, then saw Izzy's gaze travel from my hat to my heavy sweater to my parka. "I only heard it was threatening," I explained. "But I can't talk now. I—um—have a date."

Her finely shaped eyebrows arched up. Obviously I wasn't dressed for a date . . . unless it involved some serious outdoor activity by moonlight.

Then, with incredible timing, my cell phone rang.

"Your date!" Izzy suggested as I answered it.

"It's me. Nathan!"

"Oh, hi there!" I tried to sound breezy. "I was hoping you'd call."

"You were?" He sounded totally perplexed. He was silent a beat, and then, "Oh, you're not alone."

"No, no, not at all." I tried to sound light and frivolous, but my stomach was churning. I couldn't let Izzy know I had figured out that she was at least half of the scam team. That she knew where Bess and George were.

"I figured out why the UFOs appear over that meadow. There's an experimental house built into the side of a hill—"

I cut him off. I didn't know how long I could fake this conversation, and Izzy gave no sign she intended to leave me alone in the hall. "I know about it, actually."

"Oh." He paused. "Do you know who rented it recently?"

"No," I responded excitedly, and managed what I hoped was a coy smile. "Tell me all about it."

"A guy from California who's part of the *Reel TV* crew."

Lightmaster, of course. I could barely keep my expression neutral. "Isn't that great? You'll have to give me every last detail when I meet you for dinner."

"Dinner? Oh—yes. Well, I'll go right over there now and check the place out. If we miss each other, I'll find you somehow. You'll know I'm around by my whistle." He demonstrated into the phone, and nearly blew out my eardrum in the process. Finally he stopped and asked, "Do you know how to get there?"

"I think so."

Nathan briefly gave me directions that more or less jibed with what I'd figured out from the map. He told me he'd be driving Addie's truck, as he had no car of his own. He'd wait at the scenic overlook. Then I snapped my phone shut and tried to look apologetic as I said to Izzy, "My date. He got held up. I'm going to meet him now."

I half expected Izzy to try to delay me. Instead she said, "Have fun, then," and walked back toward her room.

As I walked to the car, the snow was already falling, thick and heavy. Before I left the lot, I took out the laptop and googled Frankie Lee's name. His website popped up instantly. He wasn't only an award-winning cameraman, he was one of the top special effects people in Hollywood. He was based in LA and was single; without a family, he sure didn't need to rent a large house for the duration of the *Reel TV* shoot. A secluded house in the middle of a meadow was ideal for someone like him—and for working a UFO scam. He had the *perfect* credentials to be the culprit.

I was sure of it: Frankie Lee was Lightmaster.

Nathan's directions were good. As I neared the turnoff for the house, my headlights lit up a nicely lettered sign on a post next to the mailbox: UNDER HILL HOUSE. An arrow pointed to a driveway. I drove a bit farther, and pulled into the scenic overlook where Nathan said he'd be waiting. When I arrived, however, there was no Nathan, and no pickup truck. I figured the snowstorm had slowed him down.

I gave him a couple of minutes, but I couldn't just sit, doing nothing. I got out, yanked my hat down over my ears, and started up the long, steep driveway.

The surface was slick, and the wind-whipped snow blurred my vision, but eventually I reached the top. Once there, I expected to find some sort of building—perhaps a garage—to orient me as to where the entrance to the house might be. Instead the blacktop ended in a snowy field. If there were outbuildings anywhere, the architect had cleverly hidden them. I shielded my eyes from the wind and squinted. Suddenly I spied a light that seemed to float up from underground. A window, I realized—and someone was home. Slipping and sliding, I made my way toward the window and peered inside. Interior steps led down into what looked like a cozy but spacious living room. I figured the steps must lead from the outdoor entrance—which should be somewhere to my left.

Behind me I heard the sound of boots crunching on the ice.

"Nathan," I whispered, and turned around.

A scream rose to my lips as I encountered a masked figure. It towered over me, its alien features twisted and cruel. Its clawlike hand gripped something long and heavy. I watched spellbound as it lifted its arm, which then seemed to move downward toward me in slow motion. I tried to duck. Too late, I realized in horror, as the world went black.

16

Lightmaster

Nancy. Nancy. Are you alive?"

I opened my eyes. "Bess?" My words came out slurred, and my mouth felt as if I'd chewed on a ball of wool.

Why did Bess look so worried? Then I realized—it was Bess! "Bess, you're okay." I sat up, and my stomach lurched. I thought I might throw up.

I managed to contain my stomach, but the sudden movement made the dimly lit room spin. In a moment the dizziness passed, leaving me aware of a pounding headache.

Beneath my palms the floor felt damp and cold. Cement, I realized. The room was lit by a single very low-watt lightbulb that cast deep shadows on everything.

"What happened?" I asked as Bess rubbed my back.

"Someone bopped you over the head."

The image of that twisted horrible mask flashed before my eyes. Then I remembered. "It was tall."

"Very," Bess said as I tried to work the crick out of my neck. It was then that I spotted George. She was lying in the corner and resembled a limp bundle of rags.

"George," I cried out. I struggled to my feet. After a few steps I found my balance and made my way toward her. Even in the dim light I could see she looked extremely pale. I knelt and rubbed her wrists.

"She got clobbered worse than you." Bess sounded frightened. "She'll be all right, won't she?"

As if hearing Bess's question, George stirred and moaned.

Bess sighed with relief. "That's the first time she's moved since they brought her here."

"I bet she has a concussion," I said, shaking George gently. "Hey, Fayne, wake up. You can't sleep, not now. It's bad for you."

"Tired," George muttered.

"Me too, but you can't afford to be." With Bess's help I eased George up into a sitting position. She opened her eyes and groaned. "My head hurts."

"It should," Bess said. She got up and brought over a small plastic bottle of spring water. She opened it. "Drink some of this, George."

Apparently our captors didn't want us to die of thirst.

"What about Aldwin and the dog?" I asked, suddenly realizing we three seemed to be alone.

"They aren't here?" George sounded surprised.

Bess shook her head. "They must be hidden somewhere else." Then Bess told us she hadn't been hit on the head, but smothered with what sounded to me like ether. "I woke up here," she concluded, "feeling queasy, but I barely had a headache. Last thing I remembered doing before that was going out to the Dumpster behind the café to put out the trash."

"Did you see who grabbed you?" I asked, getting up and slowly walking around. Moving helped clear my head. If we were ever to get out of wherever we were, I needed my wits about me.

"I never saw them. I think there were two men, though. One voice sounded a lot like the mayor's."

"I remember that too," George contributed. Holding on to my arm, she struggled to her feet. She tenderly rubbed the back of her head. "Ouch," she exclaimed, and then held out her hand. It was covered with blood.

"You're bleeding," Bess gasped.

"I'm okay," George insisted, but she sat back down.

George was hurting more than she let on. I sensed she needed medical help, fast. First, though, we had to get out of there.

"When do they bring you food?" I asked Bess. Maybe that would be an opportunity for us to over-come our captor.

"I don't know. I mean, I've only been here a few hours. They brought it once."

"Who was it?" George asked.

Bess shrugged. "They wear masks. One was a man, though. I know that much. Tall, too."

I looked around. Whoever was keeping us had made off with most of my stuff, including my backpack with George's computer in it. When I checked the pockets of my parka, I realized they'd taken my cell phone, too.

I felt my way around the room, seeking a way out. One wall was filled with tall metal shelves that appeared to be empty. Since the room even had a small half bath, I figured it was the basement of the house and not a root cellar. I worked my way back to George and Bess and told them about Under Hill House, Frankie the cameraman, and Izzy's treachery.

"I can't believe they went that far just to get foot-age for a show," Bess remarked.

"I can. Ratings drive the TV money game," George said. "Still, kidnapping goes far beyond a prank. And I'm worried about Aldwin and Sherlock. What ever happened to them?"

I had no idea, but I had a very bad feeling about what might happen to us. "Look, we've got to get out of here. There must be a door, a window—*something*, somewhere."

"Oh, there's a door all right," Bess said. "Check it out if you want. I tried to open it earlier. Whatever it's made of, I can't get it to budge." Bess helped me feel my way along one of the walls. Finally my hands encountered the door. As Bess had said, it was locked, and too sturdy to knock down. Without a credit card or my penknife, any attempt to open it would have been futile.

I began to lose heart. Knowing George needed help, however, made me determined to find a way out. Some instinct prompted me to check out that shelving unit more carefully. I ran my hands over the shelves. At first I found nothing but dust and cobwebs. But then, as I reached up higher, my hand encountered something cold and metal. A toolbox, I realized.

"Bess, we're in luck. Come over here and help." I picked up the box and wanted to cheer. It was heavy—probably full of tools.

I handed it to Bess. She put the box under the light and opened it.

"Whoever cleaned this place out for rentals must have missed it. It was on a high shelf," I told her.

Bess quickly rummaged in the box, then looked up, grinning. "That door has met its match," she declared. Armed with a claw hammer, a short crow-bar, and screwdrivers, she set to work on the door.

"Be quiet. We don't know who's around," I warned.

"Not to worry," Bess said. She tapped a slim piece of metal between the door and the door frame. Then, slowly, she worked it up toward the lock. A second later we heard a satisfying click, and with a twist of the heavy handle the door swung open to reveal a staircase.

Bess and I went back and helped George to her feet, then went through the door. A decidedly colder draft of air blew through the room.

With Bess on one side of her and me on the other, George slowly negotiated the narrow earthen steps. At the top of the stairs our way was barred by another door. When I pushed this door, it yielded easily and opened onto a swirl of snow and wind. Icy pellets stabbed at my face. I shielded my eyes, but the cold air felt wonderful.

"We're outside!" Bess sounded overjoyed.

George sounded glum. "Yeah—in the middle of a blizzard."

"This from a wannabe ski bum?" I forced a cheerful tone. I was shivering and exhausted, but hopeful that we'd get out of this okay. "Think of skiing," I told George.

No one seemed to be around as we made our way through the snow, heading straight for the forest. Halfway there, I heard a low whistle. Nathan's signal.

A second later he emerged from the woods, carrying a small flashlight. "Where have you been?" he asked, but before I could answer, he noticed George. By now Bess and I were practically holding her up. "That girl needs a doctor," he said. "We'd better get out of here," he added. He told us he'd seen Izzy's car pull up, which is why he'd continued driving by the house. He'd arrived only a little while ago and had been surprised to find my car and not me.

"You had me on the verge of a heart attack there, Nancy, at least for a few minutes."

"Not to worry. I can take care of myself," I said, sounding tougher than I felt at the moment.

Nathan shrugged. "I'm parked half a mile away. Can she make it?" He jerked his head back toward George.

"With you and Bess helping," George said, "yes."

I took Nathan aside. "I'm going to stick around here and investigate. Please take George and Bess, and get George some medical attention. Afterward find Captain Greene. Tell him where I am, what's happening, and who's involved. But be sure you don't confide in anyone else, Nathan. I know Izzy's in league with someone in town—maybe more than one person—but since I'm not sure who, we can't trust anyone else just yet."

Nathan nodded, visibly impressed. "Hang in there, Nancy. I have a feeling this case is almost closed."

Before they left, I asked Nathan about Aldwin and the dog.

"Haven't seen hide nor hair of them," he said, visibly upset. "If they're anywhere nearby, you'd think at least you'd hear the dog barking."

After promising Nathan I'd be careful, I circled the house, more visible now in the snow. Heat from the dwelling warmed the perimeter, melting the snow some.

Looking for signs of life, I ended up circling the house twice. The second time around, I heard a whimpering sound over the cry of the wind. After a moment I traced the sound to a well-camouflaged outbuilding, set low to the ground and against a second, smaller rise.

The door of the shed was bolted from the outside. After a couple of tries, I managed to slip the half-frozen bolt. When I opened the door, I was greeted by the sight of Aldwin. In spite of a sleeping bag someone had tossed over him, he was shivering as he hunched in a corner. Next to him was Sherlock. At the sight of me Sherlock let out a warning growl.

Aldwin looked up, his gaze unfocused. At first I thought he'd been drugged, and then I realized he was just confused.

While I debated what to do with him, I knelt inside the door and held out my hand toward Sherlock. "It's just me," I told him in a gentle voice. As he crept toward me, I prayed he wouldn't bite. But it seemed he finally sensed I was friend, not foe, and he licked my finger and whimpered.

Then Aldwin spoke up, his gruff voice reduced to a whispery shred. "The aliens. They are for real. I was on my porch getting ready to look for Sherlock when there was a loud explosion and bright lights. Last thing I remember is being scooped up and stuffed in their vehicle. They've stored me here—cold storage. I've got to get back to Earth," Aldwin muttered.

"Aldwin." I reached out and touched his arm. He flinched. I drew my hand back and said, "You already are on Earth. You're in Brody's Junction, Vermont. They haven't taken you very far away at all. And they aren't aliens—they are con artists."

He didn't answer. He sank back into his corner, and his eyes glazed over. It was obvious he needed help. I only wished I had found him before Nathan had set out with Bess and George.

I had to make a decision: Get out of there pronto with Aldwin, or leave him there in the shed, alone, at the mercy of who knew what, while I cornered Izzy and her cameraman in the house.

It was a no-brainer. I couldn't leave Aldwin.

I got up and looked to see if the coast was clear. As I stood there, something brushed my leg. It was Sherlock's tail. He was limping out of the shed, and

Aldwin was following behind. He'd found a stick to use as a cane.

"Come back here," I whispered loudly.

Aldwin continued down the road, hugging the sleeping bag around his shoulders, with Sherlock at his heels.

I wasn't sure if I should follow him, or if I should stay behind and find proof of the TV crew to bring to Captain Greene.

I looked back toward the house and noticed that the wedge of light near the entrance was wider than before. I realized it wasn't spilling out of a window, but through an open door.

With the snow muffling my footsteps I crept toward the entrance. Sure enough, the door was open. Why, I had no idea, but I didn't bother to figure it out. Instead I walked inside. I hovered near the door and listened. Whoever had left the door open didn't seem to be around.

Quietly and carefully I entered the front hall. A mudroom opened to the right, and the living room was to the left. Leaving my gloves on in case I came across evidence, I went into the mudroom. Inside, the usual assortment of winter outdoor clothing hung from hooks above a lidded storage bench.

I looked inside and gasped. Here was all my evidence! First I found several pairs of child-size scuba fins. I picked one up and examined it. Patterns had been carved into the bottom—patterns that matched the tracks I'd seen in Sherlock's pen. The box also held a collection of handsome wooden stamping tools. Again, the stamps, if pressed into the dirt, would make some very familiar alien tracks.

More confusing was a pump, a nozzle, and a long tube, as well as a box full of extra-large balloons. Another small carton held a dozen or so spools of plastic fishing wire. I picked up the wire and frowned. Hadn't one of the UFO hoaxes I'd found online mentioned using fishing wire and balloons?

I pocketed a stamp, one of the scuba fins, and a fistful of balloons, hoping that would be enough proof for the authorities to get a search warrant for the house.

I had started for the door when I heard voices approaching from the living room. I slipped behind the open mudroom door and prayed whoever was coming down the hall wouldn't find me.

As the voices neared, I held my breath and listened.

"I told you to check that basement before you brought them here!" a woman's voice said. She sounded angry, and I recognized her at once. It was Izzy, and "they" had to be Bess, George, and me.

"I did," a man replied in a defensive tone. "Last I looked, two of the girls were still unconscious. How they got out, I'll never know." The accent was pure Vermont and very distinct: It belonged to Mayor Brody. So he was the town official involved in the hoax—or at least he was one of them.

"How they got out was by using their wits, Ethan. I found a toolbox down there."

"Where did that come from?"

Izzy groaned. "Who cares?" I listened to her drum her fingers against something wooden and uncomfortably close by. "I'm sure we can salvage this."

"I don't see how," Mayor Brody said.

"We can chalk up Bess's and George's abductions to pranksters trying to play up the idea of aliens among us. I can even use it on the show. Neither of them ever saw me here at the house. They haven't a clue I'm involved in all this."

"That's all well and good, but what about Aldwin and his dog?"

"Aldwin is our biggest asset at the moment. He really believes aliens came and whisked him off his porch. The poor old coot is losing it, but it helps our cause."

Listening to Izzy, I wanted to reach out and shake her. The woman had no conscience. Aldwin was an old man who might never get his wits back about him again. George's head was wounded. Bess was okay, but just by the luck of the draw.

"What about the other girl—that detective?" the mayor asked. "You forgot about her."

Izzy groaned. "I wish I could," she said. "The girl's too smart for her own good. Fortunately, she comes across as so skeptical on the little footage of her we have that no one will take her claim of a con game seriously."

The mayor scoffed at her comment. "You're forgetting something. That girl has a nose for the truth. And the truth is, the con game ended when we turned into kidnappers. We abducted four people, Izzy. Abduction wasn't part of our bargain. A hoax is one thing. I never signed on for criminal activity, Isabel."

With every word they spoke, my temper soared. I was tempted to march up to them and say their game was up. But I knew I couldn't handle both of them alone. I also wasn't sure how I'd leave the house sight unseen and go for help. And then, where was Frankie?

Just then, a hand clamped down on my shoulder.

"You, girl, are too persistent for your own good!"

17

A Big Bang

I **managed to wriggle** around far enough to see who'd snared me. "Frankie Lee!" I exclaimed, looking up at the lean man.

"What's going on there?" Izzy called out, and poked her head out of the next room. "Not *you* again."

"She's back?" The mayor spoke up from behind her. When he saw me, he smiled, but this time his smile definitely lacked charm.

"What now?" Frankie asked, squeezing my shoulder until it hurt.

"Put her down in the storage area . . . not the one she managed to get out of earlier," Izzy added sourly.

"It doesn't matter if I get out or not," I said. "With Nathan Blackman's help I uncovered your whole scheme. He's out getting the cops now. Whatever happens to me, your game is over."

"Now, don't we feel smug?" Izzy said archly. "I don't think you are exactly in a position to make threats."

"And no one's going to believe an oddball like Blackman when he accuses me of being part of a scam," the mayor said.

"Besides, I'm just making a TV show. Everyone knows that. If I stretched the truth a bit, or went in for special effects, no one will care. . . . In fact, the publicity will help, not hurt." Izzy sounded sure of that.

"Tell that to the Feds when you all are charged with kidnapping," I shot back.

Before I could say more, Frankie hauled me down a short flight of steps and into another storage room. As he dragged me over to a chair, I quickly took in the details of the space. Several shelves were filled with winter provisions. One side was stacked with bottles of water and nonperishable foodstuffs. The other side held a complement of kerosene lamps, a portable kerosene heater, flashlights, and batteries. Above these Frankie had stored his film canisters, cameras, and lots of electrical paraphernalia. Other boxes labeled EXPLOSIVES were stashed below the shelves on the floor in a corner. Part of his special effects arsenal, I figured.

Still holding on to me, Frankie reached for some rope. Then the lights flickered and went out.

For a moment Frankie's grip loosened. Taking advantage of the dark, I wrenched free, darting in the general direction of the storage room door. Before I reached it, I was knocked down from behind. I fell hard and for a moment almost blacked out. I was aware of Frankie moving past me and up the steps.

In the dark I sensed him stop in the doorway. I realized I couldn't get past him. I tried to picture the layout of the storage room. I remembered the flashlights and the camera equipment. If I could stand up and find my way back toward the shelf with the flashlights and heavy electronic gear, maybe I'd have a weapon handy to fend him off with if he came at me again.

As I tried to rise, I realized the fall had knocked the wind right out of me. I lay there, unable to get up.

I heard the thud of footsteps above me in the hall. Suddenly from his perch on the top step, Frankie yelled, "Where are you going?"

Izzy shouted something back. I couldn't make out exactly what, but Frankie let out a string of curse words in response.

"You double-crossing witch!" he yelled into the darkness. His words seemed to fall into a black hole, though; he didn't get anything in response.

Then I heard the mayor urging Izzy to get her act together and get out while the going was good.

159

The shouting stopped as abruptly as it had started, and I heard Frankie close the storeroom door.

Had he left?

I tested my legs and managed to scramble to my feet, but even as I did, a light flickered on. It was faint, but bright enough for me to see that Frankie was still in the room. He'd lit one of the kerosene lamps and was putting it on the shelf.

His back was turned. Taking advantage of the moment, I made for the steps. Before I gained the door, though, Frankie tackled me again from behind. This time I was prepared, however. I spun around and used the force of my movement to deliver a swift kick to his face.

Unfortunately, I missed. The man was athletic and lithe, and I instantly realized that he possessed considerable martial arts skills.

I did, however, have the advantage of surprise. He didn't expect me to be able to defend myself. Before he could regain his balance, I aimed another kick at his arm.

He wheeled out of the way, again out of my reach. In the process his hand flew up and bashed right into the kerosene lantern. It crashed off the shelf and spilled burning fuel all over the floor.

Flames instantly began to spread. Frankie stared in shock, then threw himself right at me. I tried to step out of his way, terrified I'd fall into the puddles of fire. But instead he grabbed me, this time by the wrists. He made for the steps, dragging me with him.

"Get out of here—now! There's a box of explosives behind that shelf," he warned in a panicky voice.

In horror I remembered seeing the boxes.

He shoved me up the stairs and out the storeroom door. "Look, we'll both be killed if that blows. . . ."

He pushed me down the corridor, then let go of my arm. I barreled toward the open front door, with Frankie close on my heels. Now he wasn't chasing me, though. We both were running for our lives.

I plunged outside and skidded across a sheet of ice several yards away from the house. In the middle of my panic I found myself thinking that the temperature must have risen, turning the snow into ice. Ice had probably brought the electric wires down, causing the outage. The thoughts were rattling through my brain when I felt the force, and then heard the noise, of a loud explosion.

Instinctively I hit the ground, facedown, covering my head with my arms, as shards of glass and dirt rained down.

A second later the rain of debris stopped, and I felt only icy snow pelting my head. I looked up. Frankie was lying a few feet behind me. I scrambled to my feet and hurried over toward him. He was lying facedown, not moving. I ripped off my parka and threw it over him.

"Is he okay?"

I was shocked to see Izzy running up. She was yelling into her cell phone, calling for the fire department. The mayor was right behind her.

I was glad that they were choosing to do the right thing—to call for help instead of running. Still, I was disgusted that their publicity stunt had turned this ugly—and I figured everyone else in town would feel the same when they learned what was really behind the UFOs.

Frankie wasn't moving. I felt for his pulse. It was there, but he was still unconscious. The force of the explosion had knocked him right out.

For some reason, though, the fire behind us had quickly burned itself out. Maybe it was because the house was half-buried in the earth to begin with? I had no idea.

"What happened?" Izzy gasped.

"What happened is you almost got two people killed with your scheme."

"What scheme?" Izzy actually smirked. "When my show airs, the world will see there was no scheme. You can't change that."

"I don't have to," I retorted. I spelled out everything I knew—about her, about Frankie's special effects know-how, about the remote control planes and the evidence of helium balloons and fishing lines and material to fake alien footprints. Then I added, "As for your show, all the footage in there is gone. As in, it went up in smoke." It was my turn to feel self-satisfied.

Izzy just shrugged. "Did you think I had only one copy of that footage? I have duplicates in my van and also in the mail to my offices in LA. As for proof of the UFOs being real, anyone watching the show will be convinced. Believe me."

I turned away in disgust. That's when I saw Bess. She was half lurking behind the producer's white van, holding a little camcorder. Behind her, looking a bit baffled, was Nathan, holding up one of the TV crew's microphones. I realized then that my whole encounter with Izzy was being taped.

Bess motioned for me to keep on talking.

"Besides," I challenged Izzy, "how are you going to explain the kidnappings? Bess and George have already gone to the police tonight."

Izzy shrugged again. "I'm sure they'll believe me over two hysterical girls."

"You'd be surprised . . . unless, of course, the police are in your pocket, as well as the mayor here."

Mayor Brody had been uncharacteristically silent until now. He looked up from staring down at Frankie, who was still pale and unconscious. The mayor had taken his own coat off to cover the cameraman.

"You can't prove a thing," he said, not sounding so sure of himself.

"I overheard everything, about how you were in on the hoax but didn't want to go to jail for the kidnappings," I reminded him sweetly as the sound of sirens pierced the air.

State police, town police, a black FBI car, and a fire engine arrived all at once, followed a minute later by the local ambulance.

Captain Greene got out of his car and marched right up to me. "You're all right?" he asked. I didn't bother to answer; I just pointed to Frankie.

As the paramedics took Frankie away, I blurted my whole story. The captain listened, incredulous.

At the end he just glared at the mayor. "I didn't think you'd go this far, Brody," he said.

But the mayor wasn't cowed. "This girl has been skeptical all along. She started out convinced there were no UFOs. How can you believe her? She's a prejudiced witness."

"Maybe so," Bess said, coming out from behind the van. She showed them the camcorder. "I found this in the van and taped a very interesting conversation that proves Nancy's right and the mayor and his entourage are wrong. Besides, I'm willing to testify that I was kidnapped by the mayor and that man too." She pointed at Frankie, who was coming to, even as he was being carried to the ambulance.

"And I overheard Izzy talking earlier. The whole scheme was her idea," I added.

Captain Greene then motioned for his men to bring Izzy and the mayor down to the barracks immediately. He asked me to go along and give my statement. Meanwhile, he confiscated the camcorder and the tape, as well as the contents of Izzy's van, as evidence.

I told Bess I'd meet up with her later. She told me George was already back at the inn, being coddled by Sarah and Winnie. Her head wound hadn't been serious and had stopped bleeding long before they'd gotten to the local emergency room.

As we stood there, a haggard figure stumbled out of the woods. Everyone gasped. "Aldwin!" Captain Greene exclaimed. "You're all right."

His sister got out of one of the police cars. She hurried toward him and tried to take his arm.

Aldwin shook her off. "No time, Addie. I have to warn the town. Those aliens are for real, and they're planning an invasion. I know. I was with them!"

Addie May folded her arms and sadly shook her head. "Aldwin Nichols, I think this time you've really lost it." She asked the remaining paramedics to take

Aldwin to the hospital for observation, and they agreed that a checkup was in order.

Nathan walked up to me, looking dismayed. "Maybe the worst crime here is that they sent Aldwin over the edge."

I took Nathan's arm. "Oh, I think he'll find his way back soon." Lowering my voice, I added, "Don't forget, he's the town prankster."

"To think last night I thought I'd never want to eat again," I declared late the next morning. George, Bess, and I were seated in Winnie's café, indulging in stacks of pancakes drenched with real Vermont maple syrup, and celebrating the very fact that we'd survived a pretty grueling experience.

George's appetite also didn't seem the least bit affected by her concussion.

"You girls have turned into town heroes," Winnie declared, pouring us another round of coffee.

"Even though we proved the UFOs were fake?" Bess asked.

"Actually, I wouldn't be surprised if in the long run Brody's Junction's being the victim of a scam— a scam, by the way, spiced up by kidnappings—did more to put this place on the map than a real UFO sighting could."

"If there *are* such things," George laughed. As the

door opened to the jangle of bells, we all looked up.

Standing in the doorway was Ellie Dorian, looking a bit sheepish. I realized that in all the commotion of the night before, I hadn't asked George about Ellie's meeting with Winnie and her confession about sabotaging the café and stealing the recipe book.

"You're back?" Winnie seemed surprised, but her voice held real warmth.

Ellie, on the other hand, seemed a bit nervous. "I told you I would be. Here," she said. "I brought you this." She handed Winnie a manila envelope.

I wondered what it could be. I had noticed when I'd come into the café earlier that the recipe book was back on the counter.

"Come on in, sit down, have some coffee."

Ellie hesitated a moment before accepting Winnie's invitation. "Actually, I wouldn't mind one of your scones as well. I sort of miss them."

From the way Winnie beamed at the request, I sensed Ellie's request for a scone was some kind of peace offering. After Winnie served Ellie, George spoke up.

"I'm going to send you one of my scanners," she told Winnie. "That way you can scan in the recipes yourself and make a copy of the whole collection for Ellie."

Ellie surprised us with a blush. "Oh, that's not necessary." She bit her lip, then turned to Winnie. "I

167

hope this doesn't wreck things again between us, but I didn't tell you *everything* yesterday."

I saw Winnie tense. Ellie hurried on. "Inside that envelope is a disk. . . . You see, I already scanned in all the recipes." Catching George's eye, she shrugged. "I don't know how to hack into computers, but otherwise I'm a pretty savvy user." Turning back to Winnie, she added, "So I made a copy for you today."

Winnie's face visibly relaxed. "That's great," she said.

Bess kicked me under the table. I got the message and motioned for George that we should switch tables. We moved to the back table, taking our coffee. It was obvious the two cousins needed to talk things out.

"I feel we really did some good here," Bess said softly as we sat down.

"Sure, but I feel like I need a vacation," George added, gently patting her head.

"So let's try again," I suggested. "But not in UFO country."

"What, no Roswell for you?" George joked.

I laughed. "I've had enough of those flying saucers to last a lifetime."

"Besides, we all know now they aren't for real," Bess reminded us.

"Or are they?" I wondered aloud.

Both Bess and George gaped at me. "You're joking," George said.

168

"Um, not really," I admitted. I told them about the sighting the night before. "That UFO was different from the others," I mused. "It made a different sort of noise, and it traveled ahead of me on a back road. It seemed to be . . . well, alive or something."

"Nancy Drew, you're putting us on." George stared at me, waiting for me to laugh. All I could manage was a weak smile. "You're serious, aren't you?" she asked.

I shrugged. "Whatever I saw, Frankie Lee had nothing to do with it. I asked him this morning when I went to the hospital with Captain Greene to identify him. Frankie thought I was putting him on—rubbing salt in his wounds. Then he said it was probably some trick of light—something about the snow and distant headlights."

"See, that's a good explanation," Bess said.

"I'll never know," was all I conceded. "And believe me, I hope I never have to investigate anything paranormal again. Give me your ordinary, run-of-the-mill, purely human nasty crime, and I'm there!"